THE ZOMBIE CHASERS

NOTHING LEFT TO OOZE

BY JOHN KLOEPFER

ILLUSTRATED BY
DAVID DeGRAND

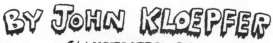

HARPER

An Imprint of HarperCollinsPublishers

ACKNOWLEDGMENTS

Many thanks to my editors, Emilia Rhodes and Rachel Abrams, for making me a better writer; to Josh Bank and Sara Shandler for their much appreciated guidance; and to Ryan Harbage and Jim Hahn for all of their hard work and sound advice.

—J. K.

The Zombie Chasers: Nothing Left to Ooze
Copyright © 2014 by Alloy Entertainment and John Kloepfer

Library of Congress Cataloging-in-Publication Data
Kloepfer, John.
  Nothing left to ooze / by John Kloepfer ; illustrated by David DeGrand.
    pages cm. — (The zombie chasers ; #5)
  Summary: "After the country rezombifies, Zack and the Zombie Chasers head out in search of a new antidote"— Provided by publisher.
  ISBN 978-0-06-223098-0 (hardback)
  [1. Zombies—Fiction. 2. Survival—Fiction. 3. New York (N.Y.)—Fiction. 4. Humorous stories.] I. DeGrand, David, illustrator. II. Title.
PZ7.K8646Not 2014   2013032808
[Fic]—dc23   CIP
                                                                      AC

       13 14 15 16 17   CG/RRDH   10 9 8 7 6 5 4 3 2 1
                                       ❖
                            First Edition

For my niece,
Livingston Pearl
—J. K.

To Mom and Dad
—D. D.

CHAPTER

A black mass of clouds churned over Lake Erie, brewing up another snowstorm as the vegan food truck sped along the frozen lakeshore toward Buffalo, New York. The entire region was still in the dead of winter despite the spring weather elsewhere. Sitting in the passenger seat, Zack Clarke watched the windshield wipers clack hypnotically back and forth. The snowflakes glittered in the weird half-light of dawn glowing behind the clouds.

The headlights flashed on a bright orange detour sign, and Ozzie Briggs steered the truck off the expressway. Office buildings with shattered windows flanked the city streets, and through the jagged glass openings, Zack caught a glimpse of the ransacked cubicles and upturned desks inside.

It had been almost eight hours since Zack and his best buddies, Rice and Ozzie; along with Zack's sister, Zoe, her BFF Madison Miller, and Madison's pup, Twinkles, escaped from New York City, which had rezombified along with the rest of the country after the original brain-flavored popcorn antidote suddenly wore off. Zack sighed loudly, completely exhausted, wishing for the zillionth time that he'd stopped Madison from eating that piece of pepperoni pizza on their school field trip so she could help them remake the antidote. But he knew that wishing wasn't going to make any difference. *Olivia's our only hope,* Zack thought.

In the back of the truck, Madison swiveled on a stainless steel stool bolted to the floor, holding her cell phone pressed to her ear. She was trying to get in touch with her cousin Olivia Jenkins, the one person who might be able to help them formulate a new antidote, if they could just track her down. "It's going straight to voice mail," she said, making an exasperated face.

"What about her house phone?" Zack asked.

"It just keeps on ringing," Madison said, ending the call, totally fed up.

"At least we know her address," Rice said from the far back, where he and Zoe stood in the food truck kitchen, whipping up some vegan cuisine. Twinkles sat at their feet, his puppy nose twitching as the smells of fried falafel balls and vegan veggie burgers wafted through the air. "You know," said Rice, "if we started cooking up some brains, we could make a killing!"

"And if we started cooking up you," said Zoe, "we could have cornballs for a week."

Ozzie slowed the food truck at a blinking yellow traffic light. In front of them, the road turned into a roundabout with a large white obelisk jutting out of the center. To their left, city hall towered over Niagara Square.

"Guys," said Ozzie from the driver's seat. "We're running low on gas and I don't see any gas stations. We need directions to the closest bridge."

"What street are we on?" Madison asked, tapping at her smart phone.

"No idea," Zack said, squinting through the windshield.

The snow flurry had grown heavy and visibility was low. Zack felt like they were on the inside of a well-shaken snow globe. Ozzie drove through the light, steering around the traffic circle, then slowed the truck down again, trying to spot a street sign.

Madison unpinched her fingers over the touch screen and a map zoomed in on their location. "I think if we go toward city hall and veer right, we can get to the Peace Bridge."

BAM! BOOM! THWAP!

"Uh-oh!" Zack said as he glimpsed into the side view mirror. "I think we've got some company!"

Two undead figures were latched tightly to the exterior panel of the truck, closer than they appeared. The zombies—one, a man wearing boxer shorts and a black puffy vest; the other, a woman in a bathrobe and pink bunny slippers— both looked as though they had rezombified in the middle of getting dressed. A mustache of snot rimed across the undead bathrobe lady's

upper lip, which curled back to show off her purplish, bloodstained teeth.

"Buckle your seat belts!" Ozzie swerved the food truck side-to-side along the roadway, attempting to shake the undead joyriders loose.

"Ozzie, chill!" Zoe shouted. "I'm trying to cook here!"

"The zombies aren't coming off," Zack said looking back. "They're stuck!"

"What do you mean they're stuck?" Madison asked, now holding Twinkles on her lap and petting his head to try to calm him down.

"I mean stuck," Zack said. "Like that kid's tongue that touched the flagpole in that Christmas movie kind of stuck."

"Ew," Madison said, and then looked back at her BFF. "Zoe, cancel my order, girl. I'm not hungry anymore."

"Uh-oh," Ozzie muttered. "Not good."

"What's wrong now?" Zack turned his attention to Ozzie, who was pumping the brakes.

"We're not stopping!" Ozzie shouted as the vegan food truck slid wildly on a patch of black ice. "Hold on!"

Ozzie spun the wheel and they swerved a hundred-and-eighty degrees, gliding toward the massive cement staircase at the foot of city hall. Zack stiffened in his seat as they jumped the curb with a loud thump. He could hear the two zombies detach from the side of the truck with a sound like Velcro ripping.

"Ack!" Zoe screamed as her batch of falafel and grilled veggies flew off the grill and onto the front of her shirt. She slammed back into the wall as the truck fishtailed and collided with the wrought iron banister leading

up the center steps of the building.

"Everyone okay?" Ozzie called back.

"Sort of . . ." Zoe sneered and raised her hands, indicating the food stain on the front of her shirt.

"I'm okay," Madison said.

"Arf!" Twinkles was all good, too.

"Not okay!" Rice yelled, pointing out the window.

Outside, the undead couple rose to their feet and tottered back toward the truck. They pawed the air, their arms red and raw from where their skin had adhered to the freezing metal.

"Time to get going, Oz!" Zack shouted.

Ozzie pressed the accelerator and the engine revved, but the rear wheels just spun in place.

WHAP! Another undead snow dweller slammed into the truck and smushed its frostbitten face against the window, fogging up the glass with its rank, hot breath.

"Yuck!" Madison squealed. "This dude's got a chicken wing stuck to his lip!"

Ozzie floored the pedal again, but the truck still wouldn't budge. "Come on." He grunted, shifting into four-wheel drive.

Madison peered out her window again, watching as more and more undead maniacs lumbered toward the truck. "Oz, if you need me to drive, just say so."

"Please," Ozzie scoffed. "We're just caught on

something." He looked at Zack then at Rice. "You two gotta go out there and get us unstuck."

"Fine," Rice said. "But only if you let me use your nunchaku."

Ozzie grunted then grumbled, "You know I don't like other people using them."

"Come on, man." Rice interlocked all ten fingers to make the universal sign for begging. "Just this once?"

"Fine." Ozzie sighed and gave up his prized possession. "But I swear, if you break them—"

"Let's go," Zack said quickly, and grabbed one of the umbrellas he'd kept from New York City.

Zack and Rice opened their doors and hopped out onto the icy steps of city hall. A gust of frigid wind blasted Zack in the face and stung his eyes. He could barely make out the zombie shapes surrounding the truck, but he could hear at least a dozen undead moans howling through the snow flurry.

A traffic light tinting everything red suddenly flashed green and a plethora of gangrenous ghouls converged on city hall from the street.

The undead congregation toddled through the storm, stumbling up the wide stone staircase toward the immobilized food truck.

"Zack, look out!" Rice shouted as a rezombified teenager lurched from behind a stone pillar and made a grab for his buddy. Rice hollered a kamikaze battle cry and swung the nunchaku at the frostbitten freak, knocking the undead hooligan flat on his back. "Dude, did you see that?" Rice asked, mesmerized with himself. "I was like, 'Whaa! Come get some! Whaa!'" Rice swung the nunchaku again, emitting a string of kung fu sound effects.

"Ozzie would be proud." Zack smiled. "Now let's focus. We've got work to do."

When they rounded the back of the truck, Zack saw that the black iron banister they had crashed into was half ripped out of the concrete staircase and the metal handrail had hooked the rear fender, lifting the back wheels a few inches off the ground.

Zack grabbed the metal bar with both hands and tugged hard, but it wouldn't budge.

"You need help, Zack?" asked Rice, flipping the nunchaku under his arm and catching it on the other side.

"No, I think I can get it," said Zack, hooking the railing with the umbrella handle. "Just watch my back."

Rice turned toward the gathering horde of abominable snow zombies. "Ya'll best back up!" he warned. "Or you're gonna get messed up!" Rice flexed the nunchaku defensively so the chain was taut. He was ready for battle.

Ozzie poked his head out the driver's-side window and looked back, scanning the zombie crowd. "What's the deal?"

"Let's give it a try!" Zack shouted up to Ozzie. "Hit the gas!"

With all his strength, Zack yanked back on the umbrella and pried the handrail off the fender. The engine roared, and the food truck shot down the steps and into the street, sending the brain-hungry truck vandals flying splat onto the sidewalk.

"Whoa!" The umbrella ripped out of Zack's hands and he fell back hard, clunking his head on the stone steps.

Rice backpedaled toward his fallen pal, never turning his back on the zombies in front of them. "Dude, you all right?"

"Yep," Zack lied, rising to his feet. A fat goose egg was already swelling on the back of his noggin. "I'll be okay."

Down in the street, Zoe threw open the truck's side door and leaned out. "Hurry up, dorkbrains! We got cousins to find!"

Zack jumped to his feet as two more zombie mutants marched toward them out of the flock of flesh-guzzling Buffalonians. The rezombified duo twisted their faces up in twin grimaces of brain-craving insanity and let out a rabid double yowl.

"*Snargle blarghle—glargh!*"

"Rice, get 'em!" Zack yelled.

Rice whirled around and unleashed two hard-smacking blows with Ozzie's nunchaku. *WHAP! WHAP!* The rezombified savages froze in place and then crumpled limply to the ground.

"Nice," Zack said stepping around the fallen brutes. "Now let's get out of here!" He grabbed his wannabe-ninja buddy by the strap of his backpack and pulled him toward the truck, away from the undead swarm.

"Go, go, go!" Zoe shouted as Zack and Rice piled inside. She slammed the sliding door.

VROOM! The food truck skidded into motion again, the back tires spraying up icy slush into the zombie faces behind them.

A few minutes later, they were driving high above Lake Erie, crossing the Peace Bridge into Canada. On the other side of the bridge, the row of customs booths

was completely barricaded. The only way through was a single booth in the middle.

Ozzie put down the driver's-side window as they rolled to a stop at the border patrol. A speed bump with sharp tire-piercing spikes pointed directly at the front fender from behind the barrier arm. To the left, a no-nonsense customs official stood in the booth sporting a black Homeland Security uniform with his name embroidered above a silver badge: T. MORAN.

"What do we do?" Rice asked nervously from the back.

Ozzie looked back. "Just answer his questions and tell the truth. These guys can tell if someone's lying. It's part of their training."

Zack took a deep breath as the border official leaned out of the booth, gazing into the car from behind his dark-tinted sunglasses. "Citizenship?" he asked matter-of-factly.

"United States," the kids all said in unison.

"Of America?" Rice added for good measure.

"What's the purpose of your trip?"

Madison leaned forward, sticking her head in the front between Zack and Ozzie. "We're trying to find my cousin Olivia. She lives in Niagara Falls, Ontario."

"Have any of you been personally zombified, rezombified, or been accused of trying to zombify or rezombify another person previously zombified or otherwise?"

"Umm . . ." The kids looked around at one another and started to point fingers.

"She was a zombie," Zack said, pointing at his sister.

"Yeah, and so were you!" Zoe snapped back defensively.

"And I got zombified twice," said Rice, puffing out his chest. "Or rather zombified once and then rezombified the other time. But it's all good. We're fine now."

They all pointed to Madison. "And she used to be able to unzombify everything but not anymore," said Zoe, batting her eyelashes for no good reason.

"That's why we need to find my cousin," Madison said.

The border official looked them up and down for a prolonged moment then shook his head. "You can't cross the border if you've been contaminated."

"But, sir," Zack said, trying to reason with the officer.

"No buts, sonny-boy," the officer said. "Rules are rules."

Then he pulled a walkie-talkie off his belt and mumbled something about a boot to his boss on the other end. A few seconds later, another voice crackled on his walkie-talkie. "Roger that." The officer turned back to the food truck. "Okay, kids. I'm going to need you to turn off the engine and step out of the vehicle."

Zack didn't like the sound of that. Not one bit.

CHAPTER

Officer Moran stepped out of the customs booth and grabbed the driver's-side door handle. Ozzie hit the auto-lock button and the officer glared sneeringly through the window. "You have until the count of three to open up. One—"

"I can't do that, sir," Ozzie said, and shifted the truck into reverse. "We're on an important mission."

"Two—"

"Yeah, mister," said Madison. "We, like, totally have to save the world again."

"Now, don't make me repeat myself," Officer Moran said.

"I'm really sorry, sir," Rice said, peeping between the headrests, "but my mom taught me never to open the door for strangers."

"Three—ahhh!"

A ravenous abominable snow zombie lumbered out from behind the tollbooth and chomped its toothy mug down hard on the meat between the officer's neck and shoulder. *"Splarghf!"*

The snowy wind howled as Officer Moran wheeled around and swatted the zombie to the ground, then sank to one knee, grabbing his shoulder in agony.

"Come on," said Rice. "Let's get out of here before he zombifies and tries to get us, too!"

Ozzie pulled a backward three-point turn, and they burned rubber back to the American side of the bridge.

They drove down the snow-covered streets, chugging south alongside the waterfront. They could see the frozen lake to the west as they moved away from the city in search of another bridge into Canada.

Madison looked down at her smartphone. "We're going in the wrong direction, Oz."

"Yeah, sorry," said Ozzie, squinting down the snow-swept streets. "I think I made a wrong turn."

As he slowed down and started to pull a U-turn, the engine screeched and Ozzie stiffened his grip, unable to control the wheel as the food truck sputtered and died.

"You can't be serious," Madison complained from the way back, starting a new batch of vegan eats.

"Did we just run out of gas?" Rice asked. "Are we stranded in a zombie snowstorm?"

"No," Ozzie said to the first question, "we still have some left, but I think the engine gave out. So, yeah . . . we're stranded," he said, shifting the gears into park.

Zack felt a shiver trickle down his backbone. He peered through the window at the frozen lake next to them. "You guys," he said. "Why don't we just walk across?"

"Walk across Lake Erie? Yeah, maybe if you live in the fictional land of Moronica!" Zoe squawked.

"I'm with Zoe on this one, guys," said Madison. "What if the ice breaks? I'm not trying to get hypodermia."

"Umm," said Zack. "I'm pretty sure it's hypothermia. . . ."

"Whatever, Zack," Madison said. "To-may-to, to-mah-toe."

Ozzie stepped out of the truck and scanned the lake through his binoculars. "Good news," he said, sticking his head back inside the truck. "I just spotted a few zombies on the lake, so it'll definitely be strong enough to hold us."

"Great! Zombies on the lake," Zoe said, rolling her eyes. "Now I feel so much better."

"Come on," Zack said to the girls. "We're right here. Everyone except Ozzie and Madison has been a zombie

before. Border Patrol is not going to let us in, and we have to find Olivia before it's too late!"

"Okay, fine," Zoe said, putting on one of the hooded sweatshirts with the vegan food truck's logo on it.

"Awesome. Let's roll, fellas," Ozzie said, already geared up with his military pack, ready to move out.

"Who you callin' fellas, fella?" Madison scowled and scooped up Twinkles under one arm.

They quickly gathered up the rest of the supplies worth taking—Rice's backpack, Ozzie's nunchacku, a six-pack's worth of Vital Vegan PowerPunch, a box of ginkgo biloba they had picked up on the road, and a couple extra one-hundred-percent vegan sweatshirts—and then set out on foot.

"OMG," said Madison as they trekked downhill through the sleeting snow toward the lakeshore. "Why is it so freaking cold?"

"It's probably because of global warming," said Rice. "Duh!"

"Well, then why don't they just call it global freezing?" Madison said. "Duh!"

"Hey," said Zack from up ahead. "Check it out!"

Not far down the shoreline, a one-story houselike structure came into view. It was situated on the waterfront next to a bunch of empty docks leading out to the frozen lake. A stack of long wooden oars leaned against the outer wall of the marina next to a few rowboats turned upside down. Everything was frosted with a surreal and undisturbed thick layer of snow.

Ozzie sprinted ahead and picked up one of the oars. He shook the snow from it as Zack, Madison, Zoe, and Twinkles caught up to him. "Now we're talking," he said, clutching the center and spinning the oar like a giant propeller.

Zack picked one up, too, and held it in the middle with both hands like Ozzie, whapping imaginary zombies with both ends of the oar.

"Okey dokey," Madison said, her teeth clattering in the frigid wind. "You dudes have fun playing Teenage Mutant Ninja Nerdballs. Me and Zoe are going inside."

"Hey!" Rice said, racing after the girls. "Wait for me!"

Ozzie flipped his attention back to Zack. "Now, you

can do one of two things with this baby," he said, gripping the oar. "First you can aim high and hit them in the temple or jaw, or you can fake high and sweep the leg out."

"Like this?" Zack asked, mimicking Ozzie's movements.

"More like this." Ozzie charged at Zack with the oar and tripped his legs, making him fall back into a large pile of snow.

"Whoa!" Zack shouted, but as soon as he felt the cold snow on his rear end, Ozzie was pulling him to his feet.

"Sorry, man, it's too slippery out here," Ozzie said, shivering in the snowfall. "Let's go inside."

Zack shook the cold out of his fingers as they entered the marina. Rice tossed them a couple pairs of gloves and coats and scarves after digging through the lost-and-found bin behind the counter. "Here you go, boys. Put these on. The girls are almost ready," he said. "They found some ski equipment in the back storage room."

A few seconds later, Zoe and Madison came out dressed head-to-toe in cross-country ski regalia. Madison checked herself out in a full-length mirror hanging on the wall. Zoe stood behind her BFF, hands on hips, looking quite annoyed. "Tell me again why you get to be pink." Zoe's ski suit was white with ugly orange and blue stripes down the sides.

"Lots of reasons." Madison pouted her lips in the mirror. "But mainly because I'm the awesomest."

Madison clopped past Zoe in her big cross-country skis and stuck out her tongue.

"OMG." Zoe scowled. "That was so uncalled for."

Madison and Zoe led the way outside in their

clashing ski suits and scooted down the snow-covered docks of the marina, the boys following close behind. The vast expanse of ice looked to Zack like the surface of what could have been some barren alien moon. Taking a deep breath, he stepped tentatively onto the frozen-over lake, and the sole of his shoe crunched in the stiff packable snow covering the thick layer of ice beneath his feet.

Twinkles frolicked out onto the ice ahead of them. "Arf! Arf!"

"Twinkles, shhhhh!" Rice shushed the pup loudly, and Zoe smacked him on the rump with her ski pole.

"Ouch, what was that for?"

"For shushing too loudly." She smirked and sped off in a burst of cross-country ski walking.

The storm kicked into high gear as they trekked out across the Great Lake. Thick clouds blotted out the morning sun, and the snowy whiteout made it so Zack could barely see five feet in front of him. He lifted his arm up to shield his face from the blustery snowfall, and then he heard a weird noise like a zombie squabble nearby.

"Globble blobble globble . . ."

"What was that?" Zack yelled out.

"You hear that?" Zoe called back.

"Globble blobble globble . . ."

"Rice, I swear if that was you . . ." Madison scolded the notorious prankster as they all slowed to a stop to listen.

"I didn't say anything!" Rice yelled into the howling wind. "I swear!"

"All right, come on, let's pick up the pace," said Ozzie, pointing dead ahead. "If we keep going straight, we'll hit the other shoreline."

Zack, Ozzie, Rice, Zoe, and Madison began walking again, pushing through the curtain of snowfall as bits of sleet pelted across their cheekbones and gusts of wind stung their faces.

All of a sudden, a monstrous figure wearing a fuzzy, hooded parka emerged from the whiteout and flailed straight into Zack. *BLAOW!*

Zack bounced off the big mama zombie's padded belly and flew back a few steps, skidding on the ice.

"Wha!" Ozzie cried, and swept the oar around, taking the undead brain guzzler's feet right out from under it. "Haw!" He made more kung fu noises and sent the fallen zombie's body sliding across the ice. Another snow zombie ambled into Ozzie's line of sight. Raising the oar again, Ozzie swept the paddle into the undead iceman's knees, flipping it upside down. The frozen fiend landed on its tailbone, hammering the ice beneath their feet with a dreadful crack.

"Back up!" Madison side-kicked with her ski and took out two more zombies in one shot.

"No, retreat!" Rice called, swinging the nunchaku still on loan from Ozzie as waves of more frostbitten ghouls shambled into view.

"No, this way!" Zoe shouted, and pointed toward what looked like a zombie-free clearing up ahead.

The boys bolted away in a flash, slipping and sliding on the icy ground beneath their feet while Madison and Zoe followed close behind on their cross-country skis. Zack took the lead, dodging left and right through the undead tundra.

"Arf! Arf!" Twinkles was gaining ground just behind him.

Zack squinted, using his hand like a visor to shield his eyes from the pelting snowflakes, when suddenly he slid to a halt, feeling slicker ice beneath his feet. *Uh-oh!* Zack's heartbeat pounded in his eardrums and he gasped. He was standing on the unfrozen brink of the free-flowing river. "Stop! Go back!" he yelled, scooping up Twinkles off the ground and turning around to warn his friends. "It's not frozen over here!"

The kids tried to back away from the freezing waters of the Niagara River, but it was too late. The zombies had forced them away from the Canadian shore, and now they were stuck at the edge of the Great Lake's frozen ice shelf.

"We just need to get over toward the Canadian side," Ozzie said.

"Which way is that?" Zoe yelled.

"I don't know anymore!" Ozzie shouted, trying to see land through the blustery snow.

"Heads up, guys!" Rice hollered. "They're getting closer!"

A huge phalanx of ice zombies was closing in around them and another barrage of undead maniacs was following close behind.

"We're surrounded!" Madison shrieked.

Nowhere to run. No way to swim. Everyone froze.

CHAPTER 3

The kids huddled together, backing away from the semicircle of undead snow creatures inching nearer and nearer. As the zombies closed in, a massive crack jigsawed through the ice from the extra weight of the roving undead horde.

A quick plan flashed in Zack's mind like a dream in the night.

"Zoe! Madison!" he called out to the BFF ski partners. "Start chipping at the ice. Hurry!"

"What?" Madison yelled.

Zack pointed to the deepening crack in the ice, then at the zombie snow-swarm. "They're too heavy!" he shouted. "We need to break away to have a chance!"

"Gotcha covered, little bro!" Zoe shouted over the howling wind and the grunting moans of the zombies. The girls went to work with their ski poles, chipping at the fissure between them and the zombies.

As the zombies converged into a massive pack, the cracking ice creaked loudly and then split in two, which sent the kids' tectonic plate of frozen lake drifting up the river. It buoyed in the freezing water for a moment, then was whisked swiftly upstream by the arctic current and floated under the Peace Bridge, where they had been just a short while before.

A few precious seconds later, Zack watched as another massive piece of the frozen lake detached behind them and began to sail in their direction. It was covered with the zombies.

"Aw, man!" Rice complained. "We just got away from those guys."

"Arf! Arf!" Twinkles barked at the undead ice floe cruising up at the rear.

The undead creatures struggled to stay balanced on the floe, a few slipping off the edge and kerplunking into the ever-quickening current. Some zombies gulped water into their undead lungs while the others surfed awkwardly on the far end of the iceberg.

With the zombified glacier drifting about twenty yards behind them, Rice bent over and started packing the snow that was covering the ice, balling up handful after handful into a little stockpile of firmly packed baseball-sized snowballs.

"Rice, what're you doing?" Zack asked.

"Come on, dude. We're from Phoenix," he said, taking aim at the undead ice floe. "How many chances do we get to have a snowball fight?" He launched a well-placed snowball high in the air that arched in the sky but plunked just short of the zombie ice floe.

"Okay, so, like, where are we going?" Madison asked coming over, totally bored with Rice's snowball fight.

Rice turned around and crinkled his forehead as Zack threw a snowball that splatted at the iceberg zombies' feet. "If my geography serves me correctly that would be Niagara Falls."

"Niagara Falls?" Zoe dropped her jaw and went bug-eyed. "Rice, that's not funny."

"I'm not kidding," he said. "But don't worry. Pretty sure we got a long ways to go before we hit the rapids and the Falls." He tossed another snowball at the zombified iceberg, which fell short again. "Darn! I was this close."

"Let me show you how it's done," Ozzie said, stepping up with a single snowball. He leaned back and brought his arm forward like a catapult. The snowball soared through the now-waning snowstorm and curved on a gust of wind before it sailed directly into the zombified face of one of the undead iceberglers.

SPLAT!

Ozzie let out an excited yelp and pumped his fist, then high-fived Zack and Rice.

Kids: one. Zombies: nothing.

CHAPTER

THWAP!

Zack's face stung as a snowball smashed against his cheekbone. He turned toward the culprit to see his big sister firing snowballs like a crazy person. *ZIP! ZIP!* Two more snowballs whizzed by his head and Zack ducked to avoid them. "Ha! Right in the face, little bro! Stings, don't it?"

Zack wiped the wet slush from his face. "Not cool, Zoe."

Zoe sidled up next to her brother and put her arm around him. "Come on, Zacky-poo, what fun's a snowball fight if you can't drill your little brother in the face?"

She pulled a snowball out from behind her back and smashed it into Zack's mouth.

"Zoe!" Zack squirmed away and spat out the snow. "You're so annoying."

"All right, you guys, chill out. We're almost there," Ozzie said, pointing to the Canadian shoreline on their left. "So here's the plan. We're going to have to get close enough to the riverbank to jump off before the current gets the best of us." Ozzie threw his oar to Rice. "You and Zack guide this thing to that side."

"Aye-aye, cap'n," Rice said, taking the oar. Zack and  Rice moved to opposite sides of the ice raft and began paddling with the current. But before they could gain control of their course, the floe struck a string of three orange-and-white buoys.

BAM! BAM! BAM! The floe careened off each buoy, spinning cockeyed in the water.

"Come on, guys," Zoe screamed, her balance a bit wobbly. "Start paddling better!"

"We're trying," Zack and Rice both called out simultaneously.

"Look out!" Madison cried, pointing behind them to the zombies. "They're almost—"

WHAM! The zombie-infested iceberg plowed into them from the rear with a powerful clunk. The two ice floes locked together, and the zombies staggered toward Zack and the gang like a crew of undead pirates laying siege to a ship.

Ozzie whirled around to face the brain-guzzling mutants. "Rice, quick, toss me the nunchaku!"

Rice reached behind his backpack and detached Ozzie's prized nunchaku. He gave Ozzie his best underhand toss, but it was way too high. The nunchaku sailed over Ozzie's head, catching a glint of early-morning sunshine piercing through the storm as they plunked into the river.

Ozzie's eyes went wide with horror.

"Arf-arf!" Twinkles chirped, and started running after the thrown object as any puppy would.

"Twinkles!" Madison shrieked and dove across the ice for her precious pup, who had put on the brakes too late and was sliding across the ice into the rollicking river. Madison nearly dropped over the side, too, but Zoe snagged her by her ski before she could. Madison now dangled headfirst off the edge of the floe, splashing in the freezing cold water. "Twinkles!"

"Zack, help me!" cried his sister. "She's slipping!"

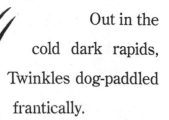

Out in the cold dark rapids, Twinkles dog-paddled frantically.

Zack quickly brought his oar out of the water and hustled over to grab Madison's other ski. Zack and his sister hung on to Madison's feet for dear life and tried to pull her back to safety.

"Twinkles, come back!" Madison cried, lunging again as the current swept her puppy farther out of reach. She sobbed and wailed, half in and half out of the water. She was still reaching futilely for her puppy when he disappeared in the Niagara's frigid current. "Twinkles!"

Finally, Madison gave up her desperate attempt to save her beloved pup, and Zack and Zoe began to pull her out when suddenly, a zombie river monster lurched to the surface and did a chin-up on Madison's waterlogged arm.

"No!" Zack screamed.

The hypothermic undead beast cranked open its mouth wide, stretching a web of thick, infectious mucus between its lips, and then chomped down hard on Madison's forearm. *"Nom-nom-nom!"*

"Yowie!" Madison cried in

pain, and pulled her arm back as Zack push-kicked the zombie in its face with the bottom of his sneaker, sending it bobbing way away from them. Zoe then hoisted Madison up over the icy ledge and back onto their floe.

"Guys, Madison's been bitten!" Zack yelled to Rice and Ozzie, who were fending off the last of the zombie stragglers.

Two big zombie oafs sporting red-white-and-blue Buffalo Bills football gear lurched across the floating ice island, their goatees frozen with snot and slobber.

In one swift maneuver, Ozzie swung his leg up in a high kick and chopped it down hard on the collarbone of one of the zombies. As the undead iceman dropped to its knees, Ozzie launched in the other direction and attacked

zombie number two with a sharp one-two punch combo.

Rice then blasted one of the frostbitten ghouls right in the kisser. Flecks of frozen slime sprung off its desiccated face and floated through the air in slow motion as the undead beast back-flopped into the river with an enormous splash.

Rice and Ozzie ran over to join Zack, Zoe, and the soon-to-be-zombie Madison, who was sprawled out in a state of shock, taking slow, deep breaths.

The river rushed audibly, drowning out the gurgling moans of the zombies bobbing in the quickening current.

"We gotta get off this river, like, now!" Zoe yelled.

With every second, the roar of the rapids grew louder and louder as the whipping wind whisked them ever closer to the horseshoe-shaped cliff ahead.

"Rice!" Zoe screamed over the wind. "I thought you said we weren't going to hit the Falls yet!"

"My bad. We must have been going faster than I thought." Rice shrugged nervously while Zoe glared at him with her signature mean-girl scowl. "It's okay, we can do this," Rice said. "We just need to create some kind of leverage. . . . Like this!"

Rice stabbed his oar into the edge of the other iceberg still riding side-by-side with their own. Zack did the same, and Ozzie followed suit with one of Madison's ski poles.

"One . . . two . . . three!" Ozzie shouted, and they pushed off with all their might. The two ice floes separated, and theirs drifted safely into a mass of tree branches at the edge of the Canadian shoreline. Zoe and Rice jumped ashore first while Zack and Ozzie carried Madison behind them by her arms and legs.

After they unhitched Madison's skis and set her down, Zack grabbed the binoculars from Ozzie and scanned the river for Twinkles, but all he saw was the water spilling endlessly over the mountainous waterfall.

CHAPTER

adison Miller lay on the beach, clutching her arm, speaking some kind of mean-girl gibberish. She sat up and slipped the pink parka off her shoulder, and pulled up the sleeve of the hooded sweatshirt that she was wearing underneath. The zombie virus had spread darkly through the veins around her bite wound.

Rice produced an Ace bandage from his backpack and started wrapping Madison's forearm.

Madison gritted her teeth and gulped back her tears. "It stings!" She groaned and stamped her foot. "Did we find Twinkles?"

"Umm." Zack panicked. "Yeah, uh—he's fine."

"Don't lie to her, Zack," Zoe said. "Not on her undeathbed."

"He's gone?" Madison screeched, and tears streamed down her cheeks.

"It's okay, Madison," Rice said. "We're gonna find the little guy."

"Promise?" she asked, and let out a small pathetic cough.

"Yep," Rice said with resolution and his fingers crossed behind his back. "Just relax."

"Ugh, I don't feel so good," she said. Madison held up her smartphone in front of her face, using the camera like a mirror.

"Fair warning." Zoe crouched down beside her BFF. "You're not looking so good either." Madison scowled at Zoe then gazed at the touch screen and watched her pale skin begin to wither slightly. Dark bags hung under her eyes, and her cheeks began to droop, making her face look jowly, like an old man's. Madison's lips quivered as she breathed heavily through her nostrils. She threw the phone on the ground and squealed disgustedly. "This is so not cool."

"Don't worry, Madison," Zack told her. "Once we reach Olivia, we'll get you back to normal like that." Zack snapped his fingers.

"Yippee!" Madison flopped backward and landed flat on her back in the snowy mud. She kicked her arms and legs out in a swift jumping-jack motion and began making a snow angel. "Thanks a bunch, Zacky!"

"Oh, man, she's literally losing her mind!" Rice said as he watched her body suddenly slacken and her head loll to one side.

"Well, she's not going to be an angel for much longer," Zack said, crouching beside her. "Zoe, help me flip her hoodie around before she reanimates!"

"Yeah," Rice agreed. "Like a straightjacket."

As Zoe leaned in, Madison's eyes shot open and she gnawed furiously at the air, snapping her teeth viciously together. Zack held zombie Madison's shoulders against the ground, trying to avoid getting bit by the undead mean girl.

Zoe pulled Madison's arms out from the sleeves while Rice flipped the one-hundred-percent-vegan sweatshirt on her backward. Zack cinched the drawstrings around the hood now covering her face, and Rice crisscrossed the sleeves behind her and tied them in a knot.

"There," Zack said, brushing off his hands. Zombie Madison was zombie-proofed and ready to go.

"Nice job, guys, but now we gotta move out," said Ozzie, strapping on his backpack.

"Wait," Zack said, and lifted Ozzie's binoculars to his eyes, peering out across the Niagara River one final time. "I want to make sure Twinkles isn't still out there."

They all paused for a moment, except for zombie Madison, who wriggled back and forth in her sweatshirt straightjacket, steamrolling her own snow angel.

"I still don't see him," Zack said, gazing through the binocular lenses.

"Poor Twinkles," Rice said. "What a way to go."

"Yeah," said Zoe. "If Rice didn't throw like a girl, none of this ever would have happened."

"Shut up, Zoe," said Rice. "I don't throw like a girl."

"Tell that to Twinkles," she said. "And Ozzie's nunchucks."

"Nunchaku," Ozzie corrected her with a deep hollow sadness in his voice.

Zack wanted to tell his sister to be quiet, too. He needed to think. Things were starting to feel a bit out of control. At least there weren't a zillion zombies everywhere now that they were in Canada. "Come on, Twinkles," Zack whispered under his breath. "No Zombie Chaser left behind." He took one last glimpse out at the river still teeming with zombies but saw no sign of their beloved pet. "I don't know what else to do." He turned and shrugged to the rest of them.

"There's nothing else we can do, buddy," said Rice.

"Except go and find Olivia."

"I guess you're right," said Zack, a single tear streaming down his cheek. "I'm really going to miss that little guy."

As they hung their heads in a moment of silence for Twinkles, a strong gust of wind squealed with a high-pitched yowl.

"You hear that?" Zack asked, his ears perking up a bit.

"I didn't hear anything," Zoe whined. "It's probably just the zombies."

"There it is again!" Zack said, listening intently.

The noise now sounded more clearly out of sync with the wind's powerful howl. "Arf-arf-arf!"

"That's no zombie." Zack moved toward the bushes along the riverbank in the direction of the yips. He pushed a few branches aside and peered over the underbrush.

"Ruff!" Twinkles came trotting out of the brambles and leaped off the ground into Zack's arms.

"Twinkles!" Zack shouted, clutching the little pup to his chest. He spun around to his friends.

"Twinkles?" Ozzie, Rice, and Zoe all gasped, triple-jinxing one another.

"Blarghles!" Madison echoed.

"Arf!" Twinkles barked at his zombified owner. The little pup was shivering nonstop and whimpering a bit, but other than that he seemed perfectly all right.

"I think he's okay," said Zack, drying him off with a spare T-shirt from Rice's backpack. "We just have to get you warm and dry before you catch a chill, don't we?" he asked Twinkles, and ruffled the frost out of his fur.

Now reunited with their canine pal, they climbed up a small slope to get back to the roadway along the riverside then strolled down the Canadian street. Madison followed them like a demonically possessed mummy, lumbering slowly and growling behind the hood covering her zombified face. The sweatshirt fabric was now soaked with excess drool, and bubbles of slobber bulged and popped off the hoodie when she grunted.

A ways up the road, the five of them took shelter at a metro bus stop, piling into the enclosed glass waiting area and huddling together on the cold metal bench. "Hopefully a bus will come soon and pick us up," Zack said, trying to stay positive.

"Here's hoping!" Zoe said as she tied up zombie Madison to a signpost.

"Well," said Rice, peering at the posted schedule,

"it says there should have been a bus here like five minutes ago."

"Aw, man," Zack said. "We just missed it!"

"No, wait," Ozzie said, pointing down the silent, empty road. "Check it out."

The kids squinted their eyes to the end of the street as a city bus rounded the corner. The bus rolled to a stop at the curb, and the kids hopped off the bench ready to board.

The passenger door opened and the bus driver looked down at them from behind the steering wheel. "What stop?" he asked.

"We don't know, really," said Zoe, and took out Madison's phone to show the bus driver the address. "We're just trying to get here."

"You're going to want the Maple Ridge stop. Then it's just a couple blocks away," he said. "You going to hop on or what?"

Ozzie climbed up the staircase first, then Rice boarded the bus holding Twinkles. Behind them, Zack and Zoe struggled to push Madison up the staircase next.

"What's the matter with your friend?" the driver asked as he raised his eyebrow at the snarling weirdo concealed by her backward-sweatshirt straightjacket.

"She's an escaped mental patient," Zoe said about her undead BFF. "She goes a little crazy sometimes."

"Well, is there any way to make her stop? I can't be having her making a ruckus on my bus."

Zack winked at his sister as he pulled out a small bottle of ginkgo biloba from his pocket. "She just needs to take her medicine," he said, shaking the bottle.

The driver rolled his eyes and waved them aboard as the mechanical door closed behind them. "Next stop: Niagara Falls!"

A little while later, the bus jostled over a set of railroad tracks as they drove up Clifton Hill. Both sides of the street were lined with restaurants and nightclubs, arcades and mini-golf courses, and haunted houses and wax museums.

"Ooh!" said Rice. "There's a haunted house called Nightmares? Can we stop?"

"Sorry," the bus driver called back. "This isn't a tour

bus, and these places don't open until the nighttime."

"What a bummer." Rice pouted in his seat.

Zoe elbowed Rice in the shoulder. "Dude . . ."

"What?"

"We have more important things to do than go to a haunted house," Zoe said. "Get your head in the game."

As they drove onward, Zack felt a surge of urgency rushing through him. They had to find Olivia and soon.

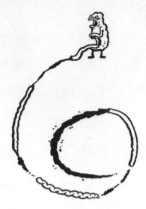

CHAPTER 6

Olivia's house was at the end of a long gravel driveway flanked by tall maple and pine trees. The house itself was the kind that might appear in a magazine. It was white with black shutters and had a porch that wrapped around the front corner. On one side of the house, a rounded castlelike tower rose up three stories with a weathervane spinning at the point of the cone-shaped roof.

Zack, Rice, Ozzie, Zoe, and Twinkles walked up to the front door. Zombie Madison lumbered behind them wriggling and grunting in her makeshift straightjacket. Zack rang the doorbell.

"The lights are all off," Zoe said, peering through the windows.

Rice reached down and picked up a pile of mail that had been stacked on the doorstep. "Some of this is from last week."

"Maybe they're out of town or something," said Zoe.

Zack rang the doorbell three more times. "Well, then we have to get inside and see if we can find something that tells us where they are."

"How do you propose we do that?" Rice replied. "The door's locked."

"Why don't we just break in?" Zoe asked.

"We can't break into their house, Zoe," said Zack.

"Listen, little bro, this is a matter of life or zombification!" she argued. "Look at my best friend, will you!"

Zombie Madison sputtered another snot bubble through the backward hoodie and staggered toward them groaning with pure animal hunger. *"Blarglesh glarglesh smargle,"* she babbled, falling toward Zack, who quickly stepped out of the way and watched his zombie friend tumble headfirst into a rosebush. Zack bent to help her out of the thorns, and as he pulled her to her feet, she kicked a large rock right at his shin and growled.

"Ouch!" Zack complained, rubbing his shinbone. "Can someone get her away from me?" Zack rubbed his leg again while Rice and Ozzie gained control of zombie Madison. Zack rose to his feet and lifted the rock that Madison had kicked at him, turning it over in his hand. There was something strange about it. The rock wasn't actually made of rock at all. It was some kind of thick painted plastic and had a latch on the bottom. Zack pulled it open. "Bingo," he said, looking at the house key inside the rock. Grabbing the dusty house key, Zack stepped back onto the porch and unlocked the door.

WHOOP—WHOOP-WHOOP!

The home alarm system blared throughout the house as they all stepped inside. Zack plugged his ears with both fingers as Ozzie started to give instructions. "Everybody spread out and look for clues. We need to find out where they are as quickly as possible. Every second counts."

Zoe tied zombie Madison with Twinkles's old leash to the banister at the bottom of the staircase then jogged up the steps while Rice and Ozzie moved through the living room.

Zack hustled into the kitchen and spotted a handwritten note on the table. It was a letter to the housekeeper from Madison's aunt with details about their vacation at Bunco's Fun World, Amusement Park and Resort.

"Rice, Ozzie, come check this out!" Zack shouted.

Silence cut through the house as the alarm shut off on its own.

"What's up, Zack?" Ozzie said, now entering the kitchen.

"It looks like we're going on vacation, Oz!" he said, showing him the note. "They're at Bunco's Fun World!"

Just then a set of thunderous footsteps sounded through the house, and Rice came whirling around the corner into the kitchen doorway.

"Did you just say Bunco's Fun World?" Rice asked with hopeful exuberance.

Zack nodded with a smile. It was a well-known fact that Bunco's Fun World was one of Rice's top three places he wanted to visit in the world.

"Oh, man, this is ridiculous." Rice did a little happy dance. "This is awesome. No, wait. This is ridiculously awesome!"

"What's Bunco's Fun World?" Ozzie asked.

Rice glared at his friend and raised an eyebrow in disbelief. "Are you serious? Do you live on another planet or something? Bunco's Fun World is like the greatest—"

"Bunco's Fun World?" said Zoe, coming into the

kitchen, too. "Isn't that in Florida? How the heck are we supposed to get to Florida?"

All of a sudden an emergency siren wailed from down the street. Zack felt a knot form in his stomach when he saw a Canadian police car speed up the gravel driveway and come to a stop outside.

"Yo, guys!" Rice said, looking out the front window. "We gotta make moves. It's the fuzz!"

"Uh-oh," Zack said. "What about Madison?"

"Quick," said Rice as he untied zombie Madison from the banister. "We gotta hide her, or they'll take her for sure."

"Over here!" Ozzie shouted, opening a closet off the kitchen pantry.

Zack sprang into action and hoisted her up by the underarms. Rice grabbed her behind the knees, and they lugged her into the closet.

"Now, stay in there and be quiet," Ozzie said to Madison, and closed the closet door.

"Grumph!" zombie Madison grunted in response.

"What do we do now?" Rice asked as the doorbell

rang. Zombie Madison thrashed and banged ferociously inside the closet.

"Police!" shouted two voices from outside. "Open up!" The cops began to bang on the front door.

"Hold your horses!" Zoe shouted at the top of her lungs.

Zack elbowed his sister in the side and looked at her bug-eyed.

"What?" She shrugged. "I don't care who you are. It's rude to knock more than once."

The four of them rushed to the front door, and Ozzie unlocked the dead bolt with a click and opened up. A thirty-something-year-old man in a Canadian police uniform stood on the porch next to his partner, a fortyish-looking woman wearing an identical police outfit. They both flashed their shiny silver badges and stayed outside, looking in at the kids through the outer screen door.

The female police officer spoke up first. "You kids live here?"

"Uhhh . . . uhh . . ." the whole group stuttered.

"Are your parents around?" the male police officer

asked, glancing suspiciously inside the house.

"Umm," Rice started to say. "That's kind of a tricky question."

"This is our friend's aunt's house," Zack chimed in. "We're, uhh, visiting. . . ."

Just then a glimmer of recognition flashed in the woman's eyes, and she punched her partner in the shoulder. "Hey," she said with what seemed like a hint of awe and recognition in her voice. "You know who these little rascals are?"

"No," he said, glaring at them. "Not ringing any bells."

"Oh, come on," she said. "These are those little whip-persnappers who fought off all the zombies."

"Well, I'll be—" He squinted at Zack and Rice and Zoe and Ozzie, then Twinkles. "You're right! They've even got the little dog with them, too."

"Twinkie!" the female officer said in a high-pitched voice and crouched to dog level. "Come here, girl."

"Actually it's Twinkles," Rice corrected. "And, uh, it's a *he* not a s*he*."

Zack rolled his eyes and sighed.

"Blarghity-blarghle-glargh!" A loud zombie noise resounded from inside.

"What the heck was that?" The male officer asked, stepping past the kids and into the house.

"Uhhh," Zack uttered, turning around, too. They followed the police to the kitchen and stopped behind them in front of the doorway.

Zombie Madison had broken out of the closet and was now Weeble-wobbling her way across the kitchen, still snarling through the gray fabric of her backward hoodie straightjacket.

Zombie Madison shook her head violently, and the hood of the sweatshirt came undone to reveal her hideous, undead face. Her eyes were rolled back into her head, blank bloodshot orbs twitching in their socket holes, and her once-beautiful skin was beginning to chap and prune.

"Is that?" The female cop asked in stunned disbelief. "But it can't be . . ."

"Madison Miller," said Zoe, shaking her head. "I know, she used to be way prettier."

"Wait a sec," the guy cop said. "I thought she was the one who couldn't turn into a zombie."

"She used to not be able to," Rice chimed in. "But now . . . I mean, just look at her."

"Look, officers, we're in big trouble," Zack said. "We came all this way to find Madison's cousin Olivia Jenkins, who we think could help us make a new antidote."

"This is her house?" said the policewoman.

"Yeah," Ozzie said. "But they're on vacation in Florida."

"So you guys need a ride, then."

"You can drive us to Florida?"

"No, better," the policewoman said. "We can get you a plane."

"You can do that?" Zack asked.

"I got a cousin in the Air Force who flies fighter jets," said the male officer. "He's a piece of work, but he owes me one. Let's go."

They all squeezed into the back of the police car and Twinkles sat on Zack's lap. Even though Madison was snarling psychotically in the trunk, Zack started to feel as though the tables were finally turning in their favor.

The policewoman hit the sirens and stepped on the gas.

"How far away is the base?" Zack asked as they cruised through the Canadian suburbs.

"Not too far from here, eh?" said the policewoman. "We'll get you all where you need to go. I'm Gladice, by the way. And this guy here is Andy."

"I'm Zack. Zack Clarke."

"I know," Gladice said. "You're famous, remember?"

CHAPTER 7

A half an hour later, they were standing on the runway of the air base. A straight-backed, broad-chested Canadian fighter pilot in a tan uniform walked out of the hangar. The pilot sauntered up to Andy and gave him a quick manly hug. Andy pointed back to the kids illuminated in the headlights of the car.

"So this is the precious cargo?" the pilot asked, staring down at them. "My name is Chet, and I may or may not be your pilot this evening."

Ozzie took the lead and saluted back, stiff as a board. "Oswald Briggs, sir. Junior Commando First Class, sir."

"Boy, you grow up in the military or something?"

"Sir, yes, sir!"

"All right, then," he said, turning to look at Zack. "I understand that you think that thing's cousin can help you make the same antidote that saved America the last time."

"That's right, sir."

"And that this particular cousin's in Orlando, Florida?"

"Yeah, but not just anywhere in Orlando," said Rice. "Her last known whereabouts are Bunco's Fun World."

Zack jabbed his buddy in the ribs with his elbow. "Right again, sir."

The Canadian fighter pilot thought for a moment, grabbing his chin and looking at the sky. "I'll take you on one condition," he said. "We do this my way. We get in, get what we need, and get out. We're not staying in the outbreak zone any longer than we have to."

"Deal," Zack said. "Whatever it takes."

A few minutes later, they were all wearing earmuffs and flight goggles as the military plane roared out of the hangar.

"That there's a Lockheed C-130 Hercules, four-engine turboprop military transport aircraft."

"Sweet," Zack and Ozzie said in unison.

In the back of the cargo hold, Rice was now busy cutting a small mouth-hole in Madison's sweatshirt to pop in a couple of ginkgo pills. He tossed a few in then held her jaw shut until she glugged down the pills.

Within seconds, zombie Madison dropped like a sack of potatoes near the emergency parachutes as the ginkgo immediately paralyzed her nervous system. Zack and Zoe caught her by the elbows before her head smacked the floor and laid her out to nap.

Zack then hunkered down on the bench in the back of the cargo hold between Ozzie and Rice to try to get some much-needed rest. He looked over at his sister, who had just lain down and was already out like a light, snoring over the roar of the rumbling plane engine. As the plane cruised to higher altitude, Zack's eyes grew heavy and he could finally relax. Almost instantaneously, he gave in to sleep and slipped into dreamland.

Zack awoke with a start to the sound of screaming and shouting. He jolted up and leaped to his feet. Madison's ginkgo coma had worn off and she had wriggled her face through the mouth-hole in her hoodie and had bitten Chet in the Achilles tendon.

"It bit me!" The pilot's voice boomed from the cockpit, waking both Rice and Ozzie from their slumbers, too. "It bit me!"

Up front, zombie Madison was rampaging around the flight deck, possessed with the rage of undeath while the pilot thrashed wildly, clutching his Achilles heel.

"You guys get her under control," Ozzie said, gesturing to zombie Madison. "I got Chet."

Zack and Rice ran forward and tackled zombie Madison, wrestling her into submission while Ozzie watched the Canadian Air Force pilot zombify at his feet. "Hey, man," Ozzie spoke to the delirious pilot as the zombie virus coursed through his bloodstream. "You're about to turn into a zombie. You have to take these." Ozzie gave him a small handful of ginkgo pills.

"Will this keep me from turning into a zombie?" Chet asked.

"Well, not really," said Ozzie. "But it'll keep you from turning us into zombies."

Meanwhile, Zoe was still sound asleep, snoring contentedly with her hands under her face like a pillow.

With Madison contained, Zack tried to stuff another ginkgo pill down her putrid zombie throat. He covered her mouth with his hand to make the ginkgo go down, but she kept nipping at his fingers with her undead chompers. "Ouch!" Zack squealed.

"Blargh! Puhtooey!" Zombie Madison spat out the ginkgo pills.

Finally, with Rice's help, the two of them got Madison to swallow the ginkgo, but the jet was losing altitude at a rapid pace.

Ozzie jumped behind the board and started clicking at the control panel, setting off an alarm.

Zoe opened her eyes at the blaring noise. "Please tell me I'm dreaming," she said, snapping to attention. "Ozzie, what's going on?"

"Guys," he said. "I got some good news and some bad news."

"What's the good news?" Zoe asked, standing up.

"The good news is we're right over Fun World," Ozzie

said, looking at the coordinates on the display grid.

"What's the bad news?" Zack questioned.

"The bad news is we're going down."

BLAOW! An explosion erupted on the left side of the jet by the wing, and Zack could see smoke through the window. The plane jerked in midair to one side, and Chet the Canadian fighter pilot rolled out of the cockpit and into the back.

"Somebody help me get this dude into that seat over there!" Ozzie yelled over the explosion.

Ozzie and Zack grabbed the unconscious pilot and propped him up in the ejector seat, equipped with a self-deploying parachute. As they strapped Chet in the seat, his eyes popped open with blank, white ferocity and he clacked his teeth, biting at the air.

"Whoa." Zack flinched back and Ozzie immediately hit the release button. The top of the cockpit flipped open, and the seat shot up into the sky. Zack and Ozzie watched in the windy vortex of the open-air cockpit as the parachute deployed and the zombie pilot floated down into the clouds.

"Okay, our boy's safe. Now everybody grab a parachute vest," Ozzie said, cracking open the emergency glass case. "We're about to be over Bunco's. I've set the coordinates of the plane to land in the Atlantic, but we're going to have to jump into Fun World."

Zoe grimaced, still a little groggy from sleep. "That doesn't sound fun at all!"

Ozzie showed them all very quickly how to put on their parachutes as the fighter jet descended over their destination. "After you jump from the plane, count to ten Mississippi and then pull the rip cord. Got it?"

"Got it." Zoe strapped her conked-out zombie BFF to her chest, ready to tandem jump out of the plane.

"On the count of five," Ozzie said, fastening his flight goggles into place. "Five!"

"Four," Zack said nervously.

"Three." Rice's eyes gleamed, ready for his first ever skydive.

"Arf!" Twinkles barked from Zack's parachute pack.

"One!" Zoe said quickly, and leaped through a passing cloud.

"Hey, you skipped two!" Zack said, but Ozzie was already jumping, followed by Rice.

"Cowabunga!" Rice's voice trailed off as he went free-falling through the air.

Zack's stomach sank to his feet. He closed his eyes then jumped out of the jet plane with Twinkles, bug-eyed, peering out of the pocket of his pack.

One Mississippi.

Two Mississippi.

Three Mississippi.

CHAPTER

The warm Florida wind battered Zack's face as his speed multiplied by the force of gravity per second. *Eight Mississippi.* A squeal from Twinkles blended with the air whooshing past their falling bodies. *Nine Mississippi.*

Out of the corner of his eye, Zack could see Rice Superman-ing through the open sky like a pro, then in a blink he lost sight of his friend. *Ten Mississippi.* Zack yanked the cord like Ozzie had told them, and the parachute discharged skyward, catching the breeze with a jolt.

Zack and Twinkles floated over the Florida

peninsula. A bird's-eye view of Fun World appeared beneath them as if they had been dropped into a board game come to life.

But it wasn't a game. And Zack knew it. This was a matter of life and eternal zombification: the living versus the undead. One misstep and humanity would be history.

He zoomed over the zombie hot zone and landed feet first with a clang on a bed of chain-link. The parachute came down over his head and tinted everything red.

"Whoa!" Zack was looking down from fifteen feet in the air onto a complex of state-of-the-art batting cages. He tugged the parachute's tent away from him and scoped the amusement park.

From where Zack had landed atop the batting cages, Fun World forked off into three multicolored cobblestone pathways with palm trees and gumball machines lining the sides. Huge twisting roller coasters soared across the sky. A red-white-and-blue monorail system weaved its way around to the different sections. This place would have been perfect except for the sluggish, foot-dragging swarms hobbling beneath him.

Hundreds of undead freaks meandered through the park. Their baleful wails of brain-craving desperation permeated the hot tropical air.

Zack looked over his shoulder to check on Twinkles.

The little pup was just fine. His tongue hung from his mouth as he panted. "Ruff!"

"Come on, Twinkles," he said to the pup. "We gotta get down from here."

Zack detached the parachute from the shoulder straps and then took off the sweatshirt he was wearing. He pulled the drawstrings of the hood tightly together and knotted them. Then he placed Twinkles in the sweatshirt and tied the sleeves together, and slung it over his shoulder like a knapsack.

With Twinkles secure, Zack began to crawl

backward down the giant fence backstop. Halfway to the bottom he looked down. The zombies were on their way, staring up at him, snorting and salivating. He knew he had to bail now or else they'd get him for sure. He took one more step down the chain-link and then dropped the rest of the way. As he landed on the pavement his left leg buckled in such a way that he was fairly certain his knee was never going to be the same ever again. But he had to keep moving.

As soon as Zack caught his footing, an acne-faced, teenage zombie freak lurched right in front of him. The teen's nose was ripe and clammy and looked like a steamed pork dumpling. Its body reeked as though it had been sprayed recently by a skunk.

Zack dodged around the undead stinker, gagging and coughing, then dashed into the high-tech batting cages. He grabbed a baseball bat leaning in the corner. It had been a while since he'd held one. The cold, hard aluminum felt good in his hands. Zack looked at the zombie coming his way. "You're in trouble, son." He whirled around and popped the subhuman zombie stink bomb in the gut. Then he brought the bat up under the ghoul's chin with a crunchy splat.

"Clickity-clap-clackow!"

Zack swung away from the fallen ghoul, bat at the ready. The zombies were converging upon him, his back against the fence. Zack ran over to one of the many gumball machines that the park was famous for. Tied to the candy machine's metal foot, a large zombified rottweiler growled and slobbered rabidly. It had on one of those plastic lampshade collars around its head. Twinkles yapped at the zombie dog.

Zack hauled off and shattered the glass sphere containing the gumballs with the butt end of the bat. Bucket loads of gumballs spilled onto the sloped pavement, and the gathering swarm of zombies started to slip and stumble.

He shouldered his way past the shuffling ghouls and found himself at a fork in the road. The zombified moans howled all around him. He had to be careful, but he wasn't scared. Fighting off zombies was one of the few things he was actually good at. Zack did a quick eenie-meenie-miney-moe then went for the center path that led into the middle of the theme park. He ran ahead in search of the others with Twinkles in the crook of his arm, doing his best not to be noticed by the zombies meandering around every corner.

Before long, Zack caught a glimpse of two familiar-looking figures up ahead. Rice and Ozzie were leaning over the control panel for a ride called The Viper—a mean-looking black-and-green roller coaster with two consecutive upside-down loops in the track. Zack waited for a pack of four zombies to go by: two undead parents with their rezombified offspring attached to child leashes. Zack crept behind the zombies as they passed and approached the Viper ride.

A huge sign for the roller coaster hung over the entrance to the waiting line with a creepy picture painted on it of a viper consuming its own tail.

"Guys, what the heck are you doing?" Zack yelled, skipping over a puddle of zombie sludge underneath the sign. "Where are Zoe and Madison?"

"We're going to ride this roller coaster and get a bird's-eye view of the place," Ozzie said without missing a beat. "Hopefully we can spot them from up there."

"Exactly," said Rice. "We're probably going to have to ride it a few times to get a good layout of the park."

"Come on," Zack said. "We have to find the girls and

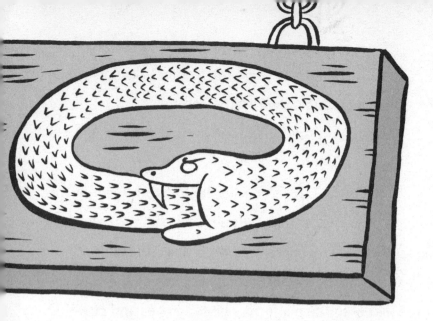

Olivia to see if she can even help with the antidote."

"Zack," Rice said seriously. "Get on the roller coaster."

"No way, man," said Zack. "I love roller coasters just as much as the next guy, but we can't just leave my sister out there in the—"

"Dude," Ozzie cut Zack off. "Get on the roller coaster." His voice was stern and serious. The zombified moans were still howling all around them. Zack spun in the opposite direction and gazed upon the high-density zombie swarm converging on the platform. The flesh-guzzling mutants had grappled over the metal maze that designated the waiting line and they seemed impatient.

"You know how to work this thing?" Zack asked as he watched Ozzie fiddle with the controls.

"Think so," Ozzie said.

"You think so?"

"Let's do it, Oz," Rice said, hopping into one of the roller coaster cars and pulling the padded restraints down over his shoulders, locking himself in place.

Ozzie hit a combination of switches as the zombies stumbled onto the platform, climbing over and crawling under the metal handrails like a jungle gym. The roller coaster started to move forward slowly, and Zack and Ozzie jogged alongside, hopping onto the ride.

"Arf!" Twinkles barked, squirming out of Zack's lap, totally spooked by the ride.

"Twinkles, come back!" Zack shouted, grabbing for the pup, but he had already pulled down his mechanical restraint and locked it into place. Twinkles trotted quickly through the maze of shuffling zombie feet and raced down a wooden staircase at the back of the platform.

"Twinkles!"

CHAPTER

The roller coaster cranked slowly up a thirty-foot peak angled forty-five degrees to the starry night sky. Below them, the zombified hordes shrank to miniature beasts ambling along the earth like voracious insects.

"Look!" Rice shouted. "Over there!"

Zack and Ozzie swiveled their heads in the direction that Rice was pointing his finger. One of the fighter jet's parachutes was tangled in the branches of a tree.

"After the ride," said Zack, "we'll start there."

"Sounds good, buddy," said Rice. "Now hold on tight!"

CLACK! CLACK! The thrill ride cranked to the top of its mountainous track and— *WHOOSH!*

Rice shrieked like a girl in a horror flick as the roller coaster shot ferociously down the steep decline. The skin on Zack's face rippled and flapped from the high-speed plunge. Ozzie whooped at the bottom as they vroomed up again into a mind-shattering corkscrew and through a tunnel on the edge of a man-made bluff. When they came through on the other side of the tunnel, the night sky seemed to swirl brightly with stars.

Then the coaster slanted upward again, and all Zack could see was the face of the near-full moon. They flipped upside down on the front end of a double loopty-loop, and Zack felt his entire stomach nearly jump through the back of his throat. As his stomach began to settle, the coaster car rumbled around a rocky bend and came to an abrupt stop, which jerked the boys forward into their padded restraints and then slammed them back hard in their seats.

The ride was over, but the zombies were quickly filling up both sides of the platform.

"Guys!" Zack shouted, throwing the restraint up over his shoulders. He spotted a clearing down the back steps of the platform. "This way."

Ozzie followed Zack and jumped out. Rice tried to do the same, but his shoulder restraint wouldn't budge an inch. "I'm stuck!" he shouted. "Help!"

Zack skidded to a stop and doubled back to help his friend, who was now under zombie siege.

"Ahhhhh!" Rice shrieked. The herd of undead lunatics clawed at the ride.

Ozzie bounded ahead of Zack and with Zack's new Louisville Slugger dealt a blow to one of the zombie freaks. Rice's eyes were bulging out of his head as he tried with all his might to lift the shoulder harness off his torso.

The mob of rezombified mutants gave off a visible wave of thick, stinking heat as the impenetrable wall of sunbaked bodies came toward Zack, Rice, and Ozzie, one ankle-twisting step at a time.

"Get this thing offa me!" Rice shouted, slamming up on the metal restraint repeatedly. Just then, one of the zombies flopped off the platform and into the car in front of him.

"Ghlarghlephlarph!"

Zack jumped into the seat behind Rice's and pulled back on the harness. He jiggled it side-to-side, trying to trigger the release mechanism, but nothing was working.

In front of them, Ozzie, with his bare hands, pummeled the undead freak in the neighboring seat. This zombie was out, but they didn't have a moment to spare.

With one last shove from Rice, the latch gave way and the mechanical restraint released. He scrambled out of the roller coaster and leaped to the zombie-free side of the platform faster than Zack had ever seen his buddy move in his entire life.

The ghouls groped and clawed their way across the roller coaster tracks while the boys sprinted off the platform and down the wooden staircase.

As the boys raced to ground level, a trio of snaggle-toothed ghouls shambled up the steps, impeding their descent.

"Blarghle!" The trio of cantankerous hellions slothed forward. They were three skinny zombie dudes in torn tank tops and Bermuda shorts. A bunch of nubbly boils blistered all over one lumbering brute's face. Another one's mug was set in a grimace of wild-eyed, tooth-baring hideousness. And the third one sputtered thick bits of spittle off of its hot, stinking breath as it snarled grossly.

"Schlarghph!"

Without missing a beat, Ozzie grabbed both hand-rails on either side of the staircase, and swung his legs up like an Olympic gymnast on the parallel bars. With one swift movement, he launched the soles of his sneakers at the chest of the zombie in front of the other two, sending the three undead brain-cravers flying backward. They crumpled up into a subhuman heap of contorted limbs.

"Come on!" Ozzie said as the boys hustled down and jumped over the twisted mass of bodies. "Let's go get the girls."

"Wait," Rice said. "What about Twinkles?"

At the sound of his name, Twinkles barked cheerily. The boys spotted him over by one of the concessions stands, licking at an old melted batch of what looked like—and hopefully was—bright pink cotton candy.

"Come on, Twinkles." Zack whistled and the little pup perked up and trotted along behind them. They jogged off through the zombified theme

park past a line of gumball machine stations on the side of the rainbow brick road.

"Why are there so many gumball machines in this place?" Ozzie asked, looking around as they took off through the undead havoc.

"Actually, Ozzie," Rice began, "that's an excellent question and I have the answer. The guy who started Fun World is like the coolest dude ever. Don't you remember I wrote my who-do-you-most-admire essay on him in third grade, Zack?"

"Sort of." Zack thought back, trying to remember. "Not really."

"Ronald Jeffrey Bunkowski started off his career in the military. That took him to South America, where he fell in love with the daughter of a wealthy rubber baron. He was wounded in combat and given an honorable discharge. He then returned to South America and wound up marrying the rubber baron's daughter. When the rubber baron died, he left the company to Bunco, which was his nickname in the army."

"Rice, get to the point already." Ozzie groaned.

"Patience, my friend," said Rice with a wry smile, and continued with the tale. "Where was I? Oh yeah. So with the rubber company's unique plot of gum trees deep in the Amazon, Bunco landed on a gold mine. He brought the Brazilian tree gum back to the United States and started a bubble gum factory, which made him a millionaire. Then he used the bubble gum money to follow his true dream of owning an amusement park where everything is full of fun. Hence, Bunco's Fun World. That's why everyone gets a free gumball with the price of admission. The dude's got a famous bubble gum factory. He even has his own cruise ship called the SS *Fun World*. How do you *not* know this?"

The multicolored brick road led the boys downhill to a gumball machine–lined plaza in the center of the amusement park. Zack, Rice, and Ozzie stopped and stared up at a gold-plated statue of the Fun World founder. A realistically carved Mr. Bunco gripped the lapels of his sport coat and looked proudly out over what he had created.

At the far end of the plaza, the Fun World resort hotel stood high above all the other structures. The front of the hotel was in the likeness of a giant gumball machine. The entrance had shiny silver doors where the gumball slot would have been, and even from a distance, Zack could see a roiling mass of zombies teeming out the lobby.

Behind them, Zack, Rice, and Ozzie heard their dog barking. They turned their heads and followed the sounds until they saw Twinkles yapping at a group of zombies gathering under a palm tree in front of a costume shop, Halloween 365.

"Up here, doofuses," Zoe's voice yelled from up above,

where she dangled from the parachute tangled in the treetops. She hung unhappily with zombie Madison still strapped to her front. "A little assistance, please!"

Zoe's feet dangled above a small horde of zombified park employees decked out in their full-costume uniforms. There were six in total: three zombie cowboys from the Wild West saloon; two carney folk from the win-a-prize games, wearing tattered jackets with long coattails; and one overly tanned lifeguard from the waterpark. They all reached up, stretching their arms out of their shoulder sockets, howling for brains.

Ozzie, Zack, and Rice spread out, circling the undead crowd.

The costumed zombies spun around and glared savagely at the fresh meat that had just arrived. *"Blaarrrrghle-ghlarghle!"* one of the Wild West zombies yowled at the boys.

A gross explosion of lumpy yellow pus erupted off the zombie's mouth as Ozzie rocked the beast with a lightning-quick elbow strike to its wobbling noggin.

At the same time, Rice ran around behind the

zombie lifeguard and crouched at the back of its knees. The over-tanned undead beefcake looked back at Rice with a perplexed expression on its plug-ugly mug. Then Zack took a running start and drilled the zombie in the chest with his baseball bat like he was bunting a pitch.

WHAM! The rezombified beast flipped backward over Rice, who scampered on all fours out of the way. "Aw, yeah!" Rice cried, popping back up to his feet. "Works every time."

"Nice thinking!" Zack said, laying out a low-five for his buddy to slap.

"Rice, watch out!" Ozzie hollered. Zack jumped back as Rice ducked out of the way of the undead carney lurching toward him. Rice then latched on to the zombie, hugging it around its leg like he was a human ball and chain. "Come on, guys," he said, wrapped around the thing's ankles. "Get 'im!" Ozzie and Zack joined hands and took a running Red Rover clothesline into the monster's gut. The zombie toppled backward and knocked the back of its head against the pavement with a soggy-sounding clunk.

Up above, Zoe was starting to seem even crankier than usual.

"What's she looking at us like that for?" Rice asked. "We just saved her butt."

"Yeah, and my butt would have been saved a lot sooner had you three not been off riding roller coasters," said Zoe. "Yeah, I *saw* you."

"We had to ride the roller coaster to get away from the zombies," Ozzie defended them.

"A likely story." Zoe rolled her eyes. "But speaking of getting away from zombies, Madison's really getting on my nerves." Zombie Madison was busy wriggling and squirming in her parachute harness connected to Zoe.

Ozzie pulled a pair of scissors out from Rice's backpack and shimmied up the palm tree. He clipped the parachute strings, and zombie Madison toppled hard to the ground, emitting an involuntary and foul-smelling belch as she landed.

"All right, you guys," Ozzie said to them as Zoe carefully climbed down next to him. "Time to get inside and regroup."

"In here," Zoe said, tugging Madison by the collar

and pulling her inside the Halloween 365 costume shop. "Come on, Biff," she said to her zombified friend.

"Why are you calling her Biff?" Zack asked.

"Because that's what she's called when she's a zombie BFF," Zoe snapped.

"Whoa," said Rice, turning around and taking in the whole costume shop. "This place is awesome!"

Zoe immediately started picking out princess dresses for her BFF and holding up options.

"Yuck!" Zoe squealed. "She's all icky!"

"Zoe, what are you doing?" Zack asked.

"Gimme a break, little bro. I'm just trying to make

her presentable. I'll pay for everything," she said. "I'd expect her to do the same for me." Zoe continued to fix Madison's hair, ignoring her little bro because that's what big sisters do best. She then zipped Madison up in a pink princess dress before painting her revoltingly shriveled face with heavy layers of rosy blush and bright blue eyeliner. Zombie Madison snarled hideously as the makeover ended and Zoe fitted a plastic astronaut helmet over Madison's freshly made-up face.

Ozzie picked up a map of Fun World from the checkout counter. "Okay, guys," he said. "At this point, Olivia is not going to be out in the open. We need to do a sweep of the entire premises."

"We've already been here and here," Zack said, pointing at the map. "So we can cross off The Viper and the costume shop."

"Hopefully the zombies didn't already get her."

"Rice!" said Zack. "Come on. We gotta stay positive here."

"You're right, buddy," said Rice. "My bad."

"We gotta turn this place inside out," said Ozzie.

"We'll go building by building."

"Well, what are we waiting for!" Zoe said, untying zombie Madison from a clothing rack.

"Chill out," said Rice. "If she's here, we're going to find her. Besides, my threads are getting pretty grimy in this Florida heat." He was already sifting through the costume aisles, looking for a wardrobe change.

"Fine, but we gotta hurry up," said Ozzie. peeking out at the ambling zombie hordes. "These Fun World freaks are starting to get curious."

CHAPTER 10

The front doors to the costume shop burst open and Zack sauntered out dressed like an Old West sheriff in a long beige coat with a silver star-shaped badge and a Stetson. Ozzie stepped out next looking sharp in a fresh set of camouflage fatigues from the Army Ranger costume. Zoe rocked a sparkly diva outfit with black leggings and a sequined top that made her look like a rocker from the 1980s. Rice of course had chosen the mad scientist costume: he had on a white lab coat, a funny blond wig, and a phony goatee. The last ones out the door were Twinkles and zombie Madison. Twinkles held the handle of the leash in his mouth, walking his undead owner.

They moved through the amusement park silently, sneaking under the radar of the zombie swarms, on the lookout for Olivia. But there was no sign of Madison's vegan cousin. All Zack could see were zombies coursing through the theme park, viral soldiers in the war to infect and devour all humanity. The undead hordes funneled down the walkways, popping out from behind palm trees and thrill rides at every turn.

Zack and the gang glanced around at the maze of game booths and food vendors. They had to be quick and quiet like ninjas so the undead hordes wouldn't detect them.

Over the din of undead groans, Zack heard a shrill human scream come from inside the nearest ride. "Hey, guys," he said. "Did you just hear that?" Zack wanted to make sure. He was beyond tired and beginning to feel like his mind was playing tricks on him.

"Sure did," Rice said. "Do you think it could be Olivia?"

"Hope so," said Zoe. "Biff's startin' to get pretty stinky." Zoe pinched her nostrils shut and made a dirty diaper face at her zombified BFF.

The Fun World Fun House towered over them. The entrance to the thrill ride was a brightly colored facade of flashing neon signs pointing to the entrance, where a rainbow-colored doorframe swayed mechanically in front of two black curtains leading inside.

The boys stood in front of the entrance hesitantly as Zoe sidled up next to them. "What's the matter, boys?" she asked. "Scared of a little kiddie ride?"

"I heard this fun house is intense," said Rice. "What if there are zombies in there?"

"Well," Zoe contemplated, "then I guess it will stop being the fun house, now won't it?"

As the boys peered in the dark tunnel entrance, Zoe dragged Madison along behind her, leading the way.

Once inside, the darkness receded as strobe lights flashed around every turn. Creepy sound effects played over the loudspeaker: cackles and wind and feline hisses. Zack, Ozzie, Rice, Twinkles, and zombie Madison crowded in behind Zoe.

"This is so cool!" Rice said too loudly as they progressed slowly through the spooky fun house.

"Olivia!" Zoe called out in a strained whisper.

"Eeeeeeee!" An identical scream to the one they'd

heard outside blasted through the speakers and started a bolt of fear through Zack's nervous system, followed by disappointment. The scream was not Olivia's; it was a pre-recorded sound effect.

"Let's get out of here, guys," Ozzie said. "She's not—"

All of a sudden the lights went out as if by design, cloaking everything in blackness. Zombie moans could be heard grumbling faintly all around them from the front of the fun house and up ahead through to the end.

"Somebody just stepped on my foot," Zoe said as she flailed her arm blindly in retaliation and nailed Zack in the shoulder.

"I didn't step on anybody," said Zack. "Ouch!"

"Me neither," said Ozzie.

"That leaves only Rice," Zoe said. "Watch where you're going, you little twerp!"

Zoe shined the flashlight app on her smartphone. "Where is he?"

"Rice, quit messing around," Zack and Ozzie jinxed each other, and squinted through the darkness.

"Guys," Rice's voice called out. "Over here. You have to

follow the red dot. There's a hidden pathway through here."

Zack looked up and saw the tiny red dot of light leading the way out of the darkened room. They followed Rice through the blacked-out fun house until the low strobe lighting returned and they came to a room with three doors.

Zack looked behind door number one, but there was only a wall made out of Styrofoam bricks.

Rice opened door number two and—*Blargh!* Two zombies lunged out at him. "Ahh!" Rice cried, and dove out of the way of the cooped-up goons.

"O for two, guys," Ozzie said, and took down the zombie hide-and-seekers, then flung open the third door.

Door number three led to another dark and narrow passageway with a sign overhead that read: BARREL-O-LAUGHS. As the kids entered the room, the speakers overhead blared with maniacal, cackling laughter. In front of them, a padded rotating spindle spanned from one end of the room to the other above a padded pit filled with fallen zombie fun house goers. The undead fun house freaks pawed at the sides of the sunken romper room.

"Okay, guys," said Ozzie. "This isn't that big of a

deal. Just remember, run in a straight line as fast as you can." Ozzie went first and sprinted across the rotating cylinder, no problem.

Zack tucked Twinkles into his sweatshirt and sprinted across. Halfway over the pit of zombies, he almost lost his footing on a puddle of slobber, but he reached his arms out and walked in place against the rotation of the padded spindle until his balance was sure again. With a deep breath, Zack let his mind go blank, ignoring the zombies reaching up on all sides of him as he proceeded forward and finally hopped off safely onto the other side.

Rice took off, making it across quickly until he slipped on his last step and went flying face-first. Zack gasped and lunged forward to help his friend, but luckily Rice bounced off the padding and rolled onto the platform at Zack's feet. "Whoa-ho." Rice chuckled to himself then looked up at his buddies staring down at him. "That was a close one."

"Great job, losers, but what are we supposed to do about her?" Zoe asked, nodding her head at zombie Madison.

Zack and the boys scratched their heads. "Ummm..."

"I'm going back," Zoe called across to them. "I'll see you nimrods outside." She turned around to make her way through the fun house and disappeared into the room with three doors. Two seconds later, she walked briskly back into the Barrel-O-Laughs obstacle room. "Never mind," she said to the boys. "There's a whole lot of zombies back there. What do I do?"

"Okay," Zack shouted to his sister, "hang on to the leash and shove Madison into the zombie pit! You're going to have to walk her across."

"Walk?" Zoe asked. "I thought you said you have to run across?"

"No, *we* had to run across," said Rice. "*You* have to walk across."

"Thanks, doofus." Zoe gripped the handle of the leash and pushed zombie Madison into the pit of rezombified Fun Worlders. "Here goes nothing," she said, and started to navigate the padded spindle, taking short, quick steps to keep up with the rotations while holding on to Madison as she walked through the zombie pit beneath her.

"That's it, Zoe!" Ozzie shouted. "You're doing great. Keep it up!"

Zoe quick stepped across the rotating spindle like a true champion. After she made it to the other side, they hoisted zombie Madison out of the undead fun pit and hustled into the next room of the fun house: a twisting, turning labyrinth of distorting mirrors.

Zack stood in front of the misshapen reflective glass and his midsection ballooned into a fat, swollen belly while Rice stood in front of another and watched his tummy shrink to the size of a supermodel's. "Ha!" Rice shouted, looking at their reflections.

Zoe looked at herself in the infinity mirrors that seemed to replicate the same image over and over forever. "Now that's the world I want to live in," she said. "A million me's!"

"Come on, guys," Ozzie said. "We gotta split."

"Eeeeek!" Zoe let out a hair-raising shriek as she

hustled through the maze of mirrors. "There's a zombie in here!"

"Where?" Rice shouted, spinning around. "Ahh! I just saw it over there!"

"Where?" Zack shouted, clutching his Louisville Slugger tightly. The zombie flashed in the fun house mirror. Zack took a swing.

SMASH! The aluminum bat connected with the zombie's face—only it wasn't the zombie's actual face but just the reflection in the mirror. The fun house mirror shattered, and Zack spun around and saw the zombie again. He swung and shattered another mirror. Zack saw the zombie again and wound up one more time, but Rice grabbed his shoulder and stopped him.

"Zack, chill!" Rice shouted. "That's like fourteen years bad luck already!"

"This way!" Zoe called, waving

everyone toward the passageway to the next room.

Now they were on the brink of a nightmarish obstacle course of stairways with blank empty doorframes leading to more staircases.

The fun house stairways jerked and shifted as they tried to navigate the room and little geysers of compressed air shot under their feet as they moved.

"Rice, be careful," Zack said to his buddy behind him, but there was no answer in return. He stopped at the top of the first mechanical stairway and looked back.

Rice had disappeared. A sputtering noise that sounded like the word HELP cackled in the strobe-lit room.

Zack rushed back to find his buddy, but on his first step, someone yelled "BOO!" Rice popped out of the shadows, scaring Zack as the floor shifted.

"Ack!" Zack stumbled and tripped on the bottom step, rolling over his ankle. He then felt a pain he had known only one other time before. It was during gym class last year when he'd sprained his ankle in an intense game of dodgeball. The sharp pain burned up his shin like an electric shock. Zack crumpled to the floor and let out a yowl. "My ankle!"

"Oh, man. Zack, are you all right?" Rice rushed forward out of his hiding spot.

"I'm fine," said Zack. "Let's just stop messing around."

"Sorry, man," said Rice. "I guess it's all fun and games until someone gets hurt, huh?"

Zack gritted his teeth and growled at his friend, sucking up the pain.

"Come on, ladies," Zoe called to her little bro and Rice. "Time to peace out of here. We got zombies a-comin'. . . ."

"You sure you're okay?" Rice asked Zack. "You want a piggyback ride?"

Zack laughed and then winced as he put pressure on his sprained ankle. "No thanks, man. I'll be good." He stood up wincing on his gimpy foot and nodded at Rice to keep moving.

"Zack," Ozzie said, doubling back. "Let me see your bat real quick."

Zack tossed Ozzie the Louisville Slugger as the undead throng from outside grunted and thrashed in through the fun house exit the wrong way.

Ozzie pushed up ahead, unleashing a flurry of roundhouses and well-placed jabs with the baseball bat on the undead fun house people.

While Ozzie cleared a path for them through the zombie onslaught, Rice trailed Zoe, who was tugging Madison. As they raced through the final passageway out into the hot zombie night, Zack hobbled up the rear with Twinkles by his side.

"Come on," said Zoe, pointing across the Fun World plaza to the gift shop. "She might be in there."

They ducked into the Fun World gift shop across the amusement park footpath and shut the door quickly, muffling the zombie moan and wail outside. Once inside, Zack paused for a brief moment to enjoy the zombie-free, air-conditioned bliss. Half of the lights were on, and except for a rotating postcard stand that had been knocked over, the store was mostly intact. There were a dozen circular clothing racks stocked with Fun World T-shirts, and the walls were lined with shelves of all sorts of merchandise: colorful bouncy balls, key chains, mugs, and more attire—from swim trunks, flip-flops, baseball caps, and visors to colored baskets brimming with toys and knickknacks.

"Dude, your ankle is really swelling up there," said Ozzie, riffling through his pack. "I know I've got an Ace bandage in here somewhere."

As Ozzie wrapped Zack's ankle, Rice called out from one of the aisles of the shop. "You guys! They have sling-shots and—wait a sec, what's this?" he asked, and then ran back to the group, holding up what he'd just discovered.

"What is it?" Zack asked, looking at the cell phone in his buddy's hand.

"It must be Olivia's," he said, showing them the phone. "It has forty-seven missed calls from Madison Miller!"

"That means she's been here!" Zoe said with excitement in her voice.

"Olivia!" Zack went to the back room behind the gift shop counter to investigate. "Olivia?"

Zack flicked on the light switch, but before he could step inside, the emergency-exit door flew open in his face and a zombie barreled into him. He raised his arms defensively, and his elbow knocked the flailing zombie girl square in the schnozz. Zack toppled over and scrambled quickly to his feet to face the ghoul.

The zombie girl rose off the ground, clutching her snout, and scowled at Zack. It had dark brown hair, powder white skin, dark hollows around its eyes, and black lips. Zack backed up, ready to take it down.

"What the heck is your problem, dude?" it said suddenly, tears welling in its eyes. "You almost broke my nose!"

"Whoa!" Zack said, squinting at the girl in shock. "You're not a—"

"A zombie?" the girl said still clutching her nose. "You're a quick one, eh?"

"Hey, uh, sorry about that," he said, staring at her more closely.

Right then Rice, Ozzie, Zoe, and Twinkles leading zombie Madison came running up through the gift shop toward the ruckus. They stared at Zack staring at the not-zombie girl.

"Take a picture," the girl said to Zack. "It'll last longer."

Could this really be her? Zack thought. *She doesn't really look like Madison, but she sure does talk like her.*

"Is it her?" Ozzie asked.

"Olivia?" Rice said, walking toward her to get a better look.

"How do you guys know who I am?" Olivia said, backing up slightly.

"It *is* her!" Rice leaped an inch off the ground. "Wait, are you still on the same Vital Vegan diet?" Rice asked.

"Uh, yeah," Olivia said. "I practically invented it. Why?"

"That zombie right there is your cousin," Zoe said.

"Madison?" Olivia gasped at her zombified relative.

"But why are you dressed like a zombie?" Zack asked.

"I'm not dressed like a zombie," Olivia said in her raspy voice. "It's called Goth."

"What's wrong with your voice?" Zoe asked.

"I screamed so much when everything went zombie, I lost my voice," Olivia said hoarsely. "Now I have a couple questions of my own. Like, how did my immune cousin even become a zombie anyway?"

"Long story short?" Zack explained. "Pepperoni pizza."

Olivia gasped in total shock and disgust.

"Now we're pretty sure you're the only one who can help us," Zack said.

"OMG," said Zoe, pointing at Olivia. "Your nose is bleeding."

Before Olivia could even touch her nose, Rice had taken out an empty test tube from his bag and was already collecting a sample.

"What is this nerd doing?" she asked as Rice caught the blood in the vial.

"Samples, baby. Samples," Rice said, showing her the test tube filled with red fluid. Suddenly, Olivia's eyes rolled back in their sockets, and she fainted in a heap on the ground.

"What's going on?" Ozzie said, trying to rouse Olivia. "What'd you do to her?"

"Nothing," Rice said. "I just showed her the blood and she passed out."

BAM BAM BAM! The Fun World zombies were outside the gift shop, half of them wearing nothing but their swimsuits, bombarding the windows and doors with their decomposing fists.

"Come on, Olivia," Zack said, gently tapping her face. "Wake up. We gotta go!" But Olivia's head only slumped to one side as the Fun World zombies smashed their way inside the store.

The snot-strangled grunts of the walking dead filled the air as a nonstop onslaught of delirious, phlegm-gurgling brain-guzzlers rampaged through the gift shop.

Rice crouched down and jostled her shoulders. "She's not waking up!"

Zack ran over to the beverage cooler and grabbed an ice-cold bottle of water. He cracked off the cap and doused Olivia's unconscious face.

Olivia gasped and shot up from the floor, looking at Zack and the gang curiously. "I just had the weirdest dream," she said. "There were zombies everywhere. and I was trapped in this amusement park, and then these nerds showed up and told me I was the zombie antidote, and then my cousin was a zombie, and—" She glanced over at zombie Madison, who looked back at her crazy-eyed in her princess dress and astronaut helmet.

"Ahhhh!" Olivia shrieked.

"Blargh!" Madison growled at her cousin as the rest of the zombies staggered thrashing through the gift shop.

"Snap out of it, Olivia. You're at Bunco's Fun World with your family. There are zombies trying to eat our brains," Zack said. "We'll explain everything else later. Right now we need to get out of here. Do you know any places that are safe to hide out in?"

Olivia thought for a moment and then said, "Yeah. The food court was pretty safe."

"Okay," Ozzie said. "Lead the way. Everybody move out!"

In a flash, Rice gathered up their supplies, and Zack and Ozzie helped Olivia to her feet. Zoe grabbed Madison by her leash, and Twinkles followed behind. Zack shoved open the emergency-exit door and ushered his pals outside into the night.

CHAPTER

With Olivia in the lead, they scurried single-file down a darkened alleyway between the gift shop and the fence of the Fun World go-kart track. Even though it was well after sunset, the night air was still humid and thick with the hot stench of undead decay.

"How far is the food court?" Zack asked as they turned out of the alley and into the heart of Fun World. His wrapped ankle was aching badly and he was dying for a few minutes of rest.

"It's on the other side of the plaza with the gumball hotel," Olivia replied.

Zack hobbled down the street trying to keep a low profile from the ghoulish fiends stumbling in all directions. He hid for a moment behind one of the metal supports holding up the monorail overhead. *VROOSH!* The monorail train zoomed overhead, and all the zombies in the vicinity craned their necks up to the noise.

"Guys!" Zack whisper-yelled over the noise. "Slow up for a sec."

"I know your ankle hurts, buddy," said Ozzie, "but we need to keep moving."

"It's not my ankle, Oz," Zack retorted. "We gotta get off the main street."

Out from behind the on-ramp to the Ferris wheel,

gaming booths, and snack stands, a dozen packs of undead amusement park freaks began to move toward them all at once, as if they were all operating with the same diseased-BurgerDog brain.

"Olivia!" Zack cried over the undead groans. "Watch out!"

Olivia spun around to face Zack.

"Behind you!" he shouted.

Olivia whirled back into a stampede of sunburned ghouls shuffling out from the back of the fun house. "Ack!" Olivia screamed as the flock of infected flesh-eaters nearly trampled her over.

One of the brainsick psychos frothed at the mouth and seized Olivia by the collar, pulling her farther into the undead bedlam. The reanimated ghoul lifted Olivia

by the cranium with one hand like it was palming a basketball and salivated right onto the top of her head.

Ozzie took off in a high-speed blur as Olivia shrieked at the top of her lungs. On reflex, Zack limped after Ozzie as fast as he could on his sprained ankle.

Ozzie vaulted into the air and jump-kicked, flying toward the chomping zombie behemoth about to feed on Olivia's brain. But at the same instant, something seemed to click in Olivia's head and she went into survival mode, swinging her elbow backward right into the beefy, muscle-bound zombie's solar plexus. The ghoul doubled over, but Ozzie's kick had missed its intended target and he went flying into the growing zombie mob.

Olivia then pulled a spin move and collared the zombie with one arm and yanked back on the beast's hair from behind. Zack heard a sound like a piece of paper being torn quickly in half and the middle-aged zombie's hairpiece ripped clean off. Olivia stood there holding the thing's toupee in her hand and shrieked as another zombie stumbled toward her out of the crowd.

She kicked the bald-headed brute in the rear end and it went flying back into the mob.

Meanwhile, Ozzie was struggling to get his footing on account of all the slime coating the pavement. "Help!" Ozzie cried as one of the zombies reached down and grabbed him with its sunburned paw.

Zack dashed as best as he could on his bum ankle and leaped into the brawl, ducking through the zombie footslog. He could see Ozzie attempting a reverse grappling maneuver, but Ozzie lost his footing again and the large zombie fell on top of him with all its weight.

"Ozzie!" Zack shouted as the zombie lowered its scruffy chin and opened its jaw wide, ready to clamp its toothy, bloodstained maw onto Ozzie's wrist.

"Nom nom nom!"

Zack jumped off his good foot and reached out, sacrificing his own hand to the zombie's mouth before it could zombify their most valuable Zombie Chaser. He howled in pain as the zombie bit into the meaty flesh on the side of his left hand.

The undead fiend's weight shifted, and Ozzie freed himself, hopping back to his feet. He clocked the zombie biter with a stunning roundhouse karate kick to the back of its noggin, sending it face-first into the mass of roiling brain-chomping fiends.

Up ahead, Rice and Zoe knocked out a trio of pus-slobbering brutes, clearing a path for them to escape. Olivia took off, leading the way, dragging zombie Madison by her leash.

"Thanks for taking one

for the team," Ozzie said to Zack, following Olivia, Rice, and Zoe.

"No sweat." Zack clutched his zombie-bitten hand. "We can't afford to lose the one and only Ozzie Briggs."

"That's true," he said. "But that's gotta hurt."

"It's killing me," Zack said, almost laughing. "But it won't zombify me. You, on the other hand, need to be more careful."

"Over here!" Olivia pointed the way to their safe haven.

She lifted the pull-down gate, which barricaded the Fun World food court against zombie infiltration, and they moved inside. Now in the confines of the locked-down food court, Zack could finally catch his breath and take a load off his sprained ankle.

"So, yeah," Olivia said, walking around her zombie-free haven. "This is the spot. Luckily, the food court was closed when everything rezombified. Those gates keep the stinkers out. This is only day two, so the food's still pretty good. We have electricity, running water, and refrigeration."

"Nice." Ozzie nodded his head in approval.

As everyone inspected the premises, Zack patched up his zombie bite with gauze and tape from a first aid kit behind one of the counters.

"Here, let me help you, Zack," said Rice, unrolling some more gauze. "You should really be resting with an ice pack on your ankle, too. The four rules of sprained ankles are rest, ice, compression, and elevation. R-I-C-E," he said. "Like me."

"Thanks, man. I'll try it out," said Zack. "Hey, can I see your phone?"

"Who are you calling?"

"Duplessis."

"But isn't he a zombie now?"

They hadn't heard a word from him since right after Rice rezombified on top of the Empire State Building. Duplessis was telling them to find other vegans to help with a new antidote, but their call had been cut short when his rezombified factory workers stormed his laboratory.

"I don't know," Zack said. "I'm hoping he got away in time. Besides, he said to call him if we found an alternative antidote, so we'll see."

"Did you just say you were calling Thaddeus Duplessis? The man responsible for zombifying everyone the first time?" Olivia asked.

"Uh-huh." Zack nodded.

"I, like, totally hate that guy," Olivia said. "When I heard what he did to those poor cow-pigs, I cried." She frowned and shook her head. "I'd really love to give him a piece of my mind."

"Don't do that," Rice said. "If he's a zombie, he'll probably eat it."

Olivia furrowed her eyebrows and gave Rice a look to say, You can't be serious.

"Never mind him," Zack said, ignoring his pal, "I know Duplessis is a little kooky, but he might be the only one who can help us."

"Wait," said Rice. "Don't call him yet. First we need to make

sure we've actually got the antidote."

"Yes, can we puh-*lease* unzombify Biff already?" Zoe snipped. "She's starting to chew her own lips off."

Rice pulled out a pair of latex gloves from his backpack and then uncapped the vial of Olivia's nose blood. He tapped a little onto a cotton ball and removed the astronaut helmet from Madison's head. Immediately, she snapped her rotting teeth in Rice's direction and almost took off one of his fingers.

"Easy, girl," Rice said, like he was making nice to a wild animal.

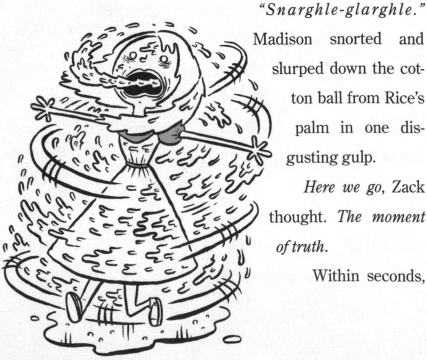

"Snarghle-glarghle." Madison snorted and slurped down the cotton ball from Rice's palm in one disgusting gulp.

Here we go, Zack thought. *The moment of truth.*

Within seconds,

zombie Madison's eyeballs rolled back into her head and she started to choke on her own tongue. Her princess costume flared out as she began to turn in circles. She whirled around and around, spinning herself dizzy until she lost her balance and toppled to the ground, knocking her head on the cool linoleum tiles with a *clunk*.

"Did it work?" Olivia asked, standing over her unconscious cousin.

A few seconds later, Madison's eyes flicked open and she lifted her head off the floor. "Oww," she groaned. "What happened?"

"Biff!" Zoe squealed with delight, and threw her arms around her unzombified BFF. "You're okay!"

"Who is Biff?" Madison asked groggily.

"You are," said Zoe. Madison looked confused. "It was your zombie name, because you're my B-F-F."

"Aw," Madison cooed, and gave her BFF a hug. "You're my biff, too!"

"Good to have you back, Biff!" Rice said, patting Madison on the back.

"You—" Madison raised her eyebrows and looked

down at Rice as if he were a speck on the floor. "You don't call me that."

Yep, she's back, thought Zack with a smile on his face.

"Arf!" Twinkles trotted out from behind Zack's leg and leaped into his owner's lap. Madison gasped at the sight of the pet she thought she'd never see again.

"Oh, Maddy, I'm so glad you're alive!" Olivia leaned down and gave her cousin a hug.

"Maddy?" Zack repeated as a smile crept across his face.

"No one call me that either," she said.

"I can't believe you hang out with these nerdmongers," Olivia whispered in Madison's ear.

"Hey, Olivia," said Ozzie. "You need to work on your whispering."

"Okay," said Rice. "Can we please get down to business?"

"What's the plan, man?" Ozzie asked.

"Hold up," Zack said, going to use Rice's phone again. "Lemme try Duplessis."

The phone rang once and then went straight to voice

mail. Zack frowned. "No dice."

"Duplessis, schmuplessis," Rice said. "Like I said before, he's probably zombified by now anyway."

"We don't know that for sure," Ozzie said.

"My point is I think I know a thing or two about antidotes," said Rice. "I have an idea, but first we're going to need some lemon-lime Gatorade, peanut M&M's, a bag of Funyuns, and some of that Spazola Energy Cola."

"Why the heck do you need Gatorade and a bag of Funyuns?" Zoe asked.

"Because I'm starving," Rice replied. "Duh . . ."

"I got it," Ozzie said. "You stay there and give Olivia one of those Vital Vegans we brought. We don't want her gingko supply to deplete." He trotted off across the food court to gather up the supplies.

"Dude," Zack said. "I hope you know what you're doing."

Rice clamped his hand down on Zack's shoulder and looked him dead in the eyes. "Listen, man. You have to trust me. Last time around, the antidote wasn't strong enough. I'm going to make sure that never happens again."

CHAPTER

Ozzie came back carrying two baskets full of snacks for the group and a case of Spazola Energy Cola.

"The key ingredient of my master formula is this." Rice held up a can of Spazola Energy Cola, a twenty-four-hour super-charged energy drink. "This is going to jump-start the new antidote and make it last forever this time! Bunco even makes it himself."

"Wait," said Olivia with a scared look on her face. "Does this mean that I'm really the antidote?"

"Yes, but as long as we have this little guy," said Rice, shaking the test tube filled with Olivia's blood, "we won't need you for too much else."

"Ugh, get that stuff away from me," Olivia said, covering her eyes. "I will seriously pass out."

"Just remember that under no circumstances can you break your vegan diet."

"Deal," Olivia said, and Rice put down the vial of antidote.

Rice turned away from Olivia and back to his makeshift laboratory. He cracked open a few of the ginkgo pills and then poured the contents into half the open containers of Spazola. He shook up the energized ginkgo blend and then added in a few drops from the test tube and gave it all another good shake. Then he came back and soaked three cotton balls with the new super-charged antidote.

"Now I'm going to need some live specimens," Rice said. "Strike that. Undead specimens."

"That shouldn't be too hard," said Ozzie. "What do you think, Zoe? You and I can go round up a couple zombies, no problem."

"We could do that," said Zoe, flexing her arm muscles.

"Well, actually," Olivia piped in, "I think I may have a few we could use already."

"Huh?" Rice turned to Olivia and gave her a confused look.

"My mom and dad and brother are all in the walk-in freezer. See, when they had all been bitten, I had to lock them in where they couldn't get me. Plus, I thought the freezer would be good, you know, to preserve them a little longer."

"How long have they been in there?" asked Zack.

"Almost twenty-four hours," she said.

"They're probably frozen stiff by now," Ozzie said.

"Well, let's go check 'em out," said Zack.

In front of the freezer, Olivia undid the padlock and pulled the big metal door open. The cold air vapor hit the kids in the face. As the mist dissipated, there stood Olivia's parents, frozen in the middle of the walk-in.

Puffs of freezing white steam shot out of their nostrils like from raging bulls in a cartoon getting ready for a matador fight.

The kids stepped inside, and Madison and Olivia approached their undead freezing family members. "That's my uncle Conrad." Madison pointed to the shivering zombie man in the corner. Conrad Jenkins stood over six feet tall. He had a thinning bird's nest of black hair, big arms, and a strong back, and he seemed as sturdy as an ox.

"And that's my aunt Ginny." Aunt Ginny was curled up on the floor grunting to herself.

"And this is my older cousin Ben."

Olivia's brother twisted his neck around with a sound like ice cubes crackling in a glass of tepid water.

The same horrific crackling sounded again as Uncle Conrad craned his neck around and looked down with a soulless, blank-eyed glare at his still-human kin. Aunt Ginny turned around, too, flashing her teeth like a mad dog baring its fangs.

They crept slowly toward the kids, who were standing

in the doorway of the walk-in freezer.

"How are we going to unzombify them?" asked Olivia, who was staring wide-eyed at her half-frozen family.

"These guys need to be sedated first," Rice said.

"Good idea," Zack said, watching Olivia's parents and brother slowly crick and creak toward them in the dark, chilly freezer.

They all backed up, luring the frozen ghouls out of the walk-in and into the main seating area of the Fun World food pavilion.

Rice went into his pack and quickly produced the bottle of ginkgo pills. He came over to the tables and started popping them in the Jenkins's hungry open mouths.

"What does this do exactly?" Olivia asked.

"Ginkgo biloba," Madison explained to her cousin. "It kind of knocks zombies out after they swallow it."

Within a few minutes, the gingko began to kick in, and Conrad, Ginny, and Ben toppled over into a deep slumber. Ozzie and Rice then picked up Olivia's dad, Zoe and Madison grabbed her mom, and Olivia and Zack took Ben over to the food court tables so they could thaw out.

Rice brought over the bowl of ginkgo-energy antidote and then began to administer it to the Jenkins family by dropping the cotton balls soaked in the concoction one by one into their mouths.

"Rice," Olivia asked, peeking through the cracks between her fingers that were covering her eyes, "do you really think this is going to work?"

"Yes," Rice said, standing back to watch. "Definitely."

Within seconds, Olivia's parents started convulsing and writhing on the tables.

"Is that what's supposed to happen?" Madison asked.

"Uh . . ." Rice furrowed his brow with a look of bewildered amusement on his face. "I mean, we're kind of in uncharted territory here."

"Well, you better get into some charted territory," Olivia shrieked. "That's my family you're messing with."

"I-I'm not quite sure what's going on anymore!" Rice yelled back defensively.

"You sure were sure a minute ago," Madison snapped.

"Well, that was a minute ago, okay?"

"Guys, stop fighting and check this out," Zack said, watching the zombie specimens get up off the tables.

"You did it!" Olivia said to Rice as her parents rose to their feet. "Mom! Dad! Ben!"

But the reanimated bodies standing up were still zombified, and somehow even more so. *"Flurghle!"* The trio of zombies wailed and thrashed through Rice's bootleg science lab.

BANG! CRASH! The re-rezombified zombies walked

forward and ripped out the tables bolted to the floor.

"I don't understand. This is not what was supposed to happen!" Rice yelled over the mayhem. Frantically, Rice examined the ingredient label on the back of the energy drink more closely. "Of course," he said, smacking his forehead. "This stuff has Caribbean sea plankton in it!"

"So?" Olivia raised her eyebrows.

"Turritopsis nutricula!" Rice exclaimed incoherently. "The immortal jellyfish! They breed in the sea plankton. The plankton must have super-charged the virus and somehow neutralized the antidote! And now they have smarter, faster zombie brains!" Rice was clearly freaking out.

"Umm," Olivia said. "Does he have an off button?"

"Unfortunately not," said Zoe. "The nerd virus is permanent."

"So," Olivia turned back to Rice. "Are you trying to

tell me that you just turned my entire family into a bunch of super zombies?"

"Look on the bright side," Rice said sheepishly. "At least they're super."

"Do you even know how to turn them back?" Olivia was starting to hyperventilate.

"We know your blood worked to cure Madison. If we can get them a dose of the antidote without the Spazola, they should be as good as alive again." Rice looked at his friends with confidence.

"Well, right now we have to stop them," Ozzie said, butting in. "Listen, Olivia. I promise I won't do any permanent brain damage, but maybe you don't want to watch this." Ozzie then rushed at the trio of super zombies and launched into a kung fu combo: right-left-right followed by a high, straight kick to Uncle Conrad's sternum. Olivia's super zombie father dodged to one side and blocked Ozzie's onslaught by grabbing Ozzie's ankle with one hand and knocking him to the floor with the other.

"Ooomph!" Ozzie hit the linoleum hard, knocking the wind out of him.

Aunt Ginny and Cousin Ben lunged for him, but he was up in a flash.

"Hey, man, hurry up!" Zack called to Ozzie as he limped quickly toward the pull-down gate at the exit. "We gotta get outta here!"

Ozzie dodged the swiping arms of the super zombies, who were maneuvering through the food court in a three-pronged, synchronized attack. He rushed away from the super zombies and ducked under the gate.

As soon as Ozzie stepped out, Rice slammed the gate down hard. The super zombies clung to the metal grate, face-to-face with their creator. Rice stared back seemingly in shock as he watched his Frankensteinian zombie monsters turn away and huddle up.

"*Blarghle blarghle blarghle*," the super zombie family communicated with one another, grunting back and forth in some crazed zombie caveman speak.

The super zombie trio then placed their decaying arms in the middle of the circle and stacked their pus-dribbling hands one on top of the next.

"*Flugh-ghlarghle!*" they chanted and swung their

arms up like teammates before a game.

Rice gasped as the trio of zombies rerouted through the food court and headed directly for the emergency exit on the opposite side of the pavilion. "Oh no, they're learning," Rice said in a far-off voice. "What have I done?"

CHAPTER

"C ome on!" said Zack, pointing away from the direction the super zombies were headed. "That way!"

"*Blarghf!*" A slew of zombie moms and dads came barreling through the entrance hall to the food court, their bare skin crispy and flaking from their bright pink sunburns.

"Okay." Zack stopped in his tracks. "Maybe not that way!"

"AHHH!" Madison and Olivia both shrieked as another zombie pack of undead Fun World children shuffled around the corner and forced them down the side hallway, leading to the service doors that went through the back kitchens. With no other way out, they retreated through the doors and down the grungy hall-way intended for employees only.

"You guys, over here!" said Olivia, finding a side emergency-exit door off an adjacent hallway. The alarm sounded a series of ear-piercing beeps as they burst out into the heat of the stinking, undead night.

Zack and the gang ran back outside into the amuse-ment park and hid behind a Fun World ice cream shack. They stopped for a moment to catch their breaths.

"Yo, man," Zack said to Rice. "What happened back there?"

"I'll admit," Rice said, putting his hands up and back-ing away from Olivia, who was scowling at him with a mean mug on her face, "it was a rookie mistake."

"A rookie mistake?" Olivia said, the anger growing in her voice.

"Come on, guys, we can't stay here and play the blame game," Ozzie said. "Those things are going to find us eventually. Rice, you said they can communicate?"

"Uh-huh." Rice nodded. "And they know what we look like."

"Well, those *things* are my mom and dad and big brother."

"Sorry, Olivia," Zack said. "I know it's messed up. We've all been there, but we have to get out of Fun World and get you to a safe location before it's too late. We'll find a way to un-super-zombify them."

As they sprinted to the exits of the food court pavilion, Zack noticed a distinct lack of zombies milling around outside.

"Where did all the zombies go?" he asked, limping on his sprained ankle.

"Who cares?" said Zoe. "Just keep up, slowpoke."

They hurried through the undead ghost town, but when they reached the main entrance, they saw a massive pack of ghouls blocking the front gates, the only way they knew out of Bunco's Fun World.

Super zombie Ben was at the front of the crowd, hunched over, prancing from one foot to the other like a dancing baboon. He seemed to be barking orders at the zombies, but they weren't listening. Ben grunted angrily and started to grab the normal zombies by their decaying arms, hurling them into the massive cluster to block off the main entrance even further. He turned his head abruptly toward Zack and the gang, and a crooked smile flashed across his pallid, undead face.

"Are you seeing this?" Madison said.

"OMG," Zoe said. "He's using them to trap us inside the park."

"He's trying to control them," Rice said.

"This is way worse than we thought," said Ozzie.

Ben pointed toward Zack and yowled a battle cry in his native zombie tongue. Zack watched as Ben's platoon of undead civilians turned and started advancing toward them.

"There's gotta be another way out!" Zack yelled, spinning around. "Let's go!"

But as Zack and the gang moved back through the park, they soon spotted Uncle Conrad sitting behind the wheel of a golf cart trying to herd more zombies toward another Fun World exit.

"It looks like they're getting smarter!" Zoe yelled.

They all watched as Uncle Conrad drove himself into the fence around one of the rides. Not knowing how to reverse, the super zombie kept driving forward into the fence. He smashed the steering wheel with both hands and then hopped out of the cart.

"Well," Zoe corrected herself, "maybe not that smart."

Uncle Conrad's head cranked around slowly as his eyes locked with the kids' gaze. Olivia's super zombie pops then lifted the golf cart off the ground, aimed it directly at the kids, and set it back down before getting behind the wheel and driving right toward them.

"You guys," Olivia said, quickly dragging Zack away, "we just need to get to the w a t e r p a r k . There's a parking lot on the other side of the fence there, and if we can get over the fence, we can get to my parents' rental car."

"Good idea, Olivia!" said Zack. "But we're going to have to get through these guys first."

Waves of moaning zombies surged toward them down the main thoroughfare and up the rainbow brick road.

"Over here!" Rice shouted, pointing toward the Fun World go-kart tracks.

Zack, Rice, Ozzie, Zoe, Madison, Olivia, and Twinkles raced through the gates. Ozzie jumped behind the check-in counter and started tossing everyone helmets. Then they hopped in the go-karts and buckled up. Zack nestled snugly into the go-kart's leather padded seat and turned the key to start the motor. "Ready?" Zack shouted over the roar of motors and zombie groans. Ozzie raised his

arm and his go-kart led the way. The six of them vroomed off the track and into the fun park.

Zack steered right then left, zipping past the undead droves, swerving in and out of the zombie foot traffic.

All six go-karts banked to the right and away from Cousin Ben's crew of zombie cronies. A fearful thrill ran through Zack as he jerked the steering wheel back and forth, swerving like a Formula 1 racer. He floored the accelerator, and his go-kart sped past Bunco's statue, by the batting cages, and finally toward the waterpark.

As they cruised into the waterpark, the go-karts all slowed down amid the many water rides. Zack, Rice, Ozzie, Madison, Zoe, and Olivia threw the go-karts into park and jumped out onto the pavement. In front of them,

they could see the Double Helix: the tallest, fastest slide on the East Coast.

Rice gazed skyward, admiring the Double Helix. The giant mega-slide was actually made up of two separate slides wrapping around each other in a spiral. It was forty feet high and twisted from one end of the waterpark to the other before dropping at a sharp angle nearly straight down. "Whoa," Rice said. "Check this thing out!"

"No more rides, Ricey-poo," Zoe said. "Time to get out of Freak World for reals."

Ozzie put his foot on the tall wooden fence bordering the parking lot and then climbed his way to the top. On the ground, Zack squinted through a hole in the wood. Staring back at him, a bloodshot eyeball dripping with zombie goop bulged through the peephole.

"Ozzie, wait!" Zack shouted as his friend peered over the fence.

"Whoa!" Ozzie said, seeing that the pack of zombies led by Aunt Ginny was waiting to ambush them on the other side.

"Uh, dude," Rice said, nudging Zack away from the

fence. "We gotta go!"

Zack whirled around away from the zombified fence and looked back into the waterpark and Fun World beyond it.

Olivia let out a shriek that resounded throughout the thick, stench-filled air.

Coming toward them in the dinged-up golf cart, Uncle Conrad herded a dense, impenetrable pack of zombies, blocking their only route to backtrack out of the waterpark on foot. The super zombie jumped off the golf cart and limped slowly on his bum hip, licking his undead chops.

Behind them, Aunt Ginny's zombies were scaling the fence, piggybacking one another and flopping over inside the waterpark.

"Looks like you're going to get your wish after all," Olivia said to Rice. "Let's go!" They took off running away from the now zombified parking lot fence toward the sky-high ladder of the Double Helix waterslide.

There was only one way out. And that was up.

CHAPTER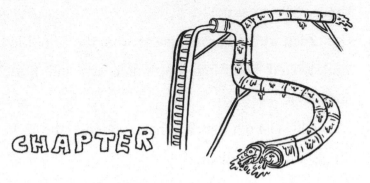

One by one they climbed up the waterpark's mega-slide. Twenty feet in the air, Zack gulped, looking over at the two twisting slides of the Double Helix. It was a long way down, but the landing pool was well away from the zombie hordes below.

Ozzie was the first to reach the top. "See ya later, alligators!" he said as he dove down the slide headfirst.

Next in line, Rice was gathering his courage to jump, readying himself with a little song. "One for the zombies. Two for my bros. Three to get ready. And four to— Whoa!"

Zoe gave Rice a good shove in the rear. "Ahhhhhh!"

Rice screamed like a baby as he went flying down the Double Helix waterslide.

Zack looked down the ladder behind him. Olivia's super-zombified dad was climbing after them, scrambling up the rungs as fast as he could.

"Hurry up, guys," Zack said to the girls. "Uncle Conrad's a climber."

The girls slid down one by one—first Zoe, then Olivia, then Madison, who was carrying Twinkles, leaving Zack alone at the top.

Zack took one more look behind him and then leaped off the platform, spiraling down the slide. He twisted and turned, shooting down the slick, hard plastic chute. He spun down the Double Helix, catching flashes of Fun World in a wild, dizzy blur. Then, as the water slide approached the dreaded drop, Zack's stomach sank to his ankles and he shot straight down into the massive pool below.

Zack bobbed to the surface and sucked a shock of air into his lungs. Ozzie, Rice, and the girls were all treading water around him. Twinkles was doggy-paddling and barking incessantly.

"Everybody okay?" Zack asked, trying not to get any of the slimy zombie water in his mouth.

"Yep!" the gang said in unison, and they started to swim to the edge.

"Yo," Ozzie said, pointing down to the bottom of the deep pool. "Keep your feet up everybody. There's zombies on the bottom!"

Zack glanced below the surface, and the waves bobbed with the distorted images of submerged zombie bottom-feeders shimmering through the pool water's dark prism.

As they continued to cautiously make their way to the edge, two waterpark zombies slid out of the adjacent waterslides at rapid speed. Swimming next to Olivia, Zack quickly ducked as one of the airborne ghouls belly-flopped over him into the water.

"Eeek!" Olivia shrieked as the other zombie landed directly on top of her.

"Olivia!" Zack cried, stopping mid-swim and turning around to see if she was okay.

The zombified waterslider plunged Olivia underwater, and she started splashing wildly in the middle of the pool. Olivia kicked the waterslide zombie away from her, and it sank to the bottom, unable to swim. But another zombie on the bottom of the pool now had her by the ankle, yanking her down. Zack swam over and caught her by the wrist. He pulled up, trying to keep her head above water, but the underwater zombie had all the leverage. Zack's hand slipped from Olivia's wrist, and she gurgled the pool water before disappearing in a sinkhole of air bubbles.

Zack took a massive gulp of air and dove down after her.

The chlorine stung his eyeballs something fierce as he looked around desperately underwater. Then he spotted her, struggling to free herself from the zombie's death grip. Zack dove deeper and stuck his fingers between Olivia's ankle and the zombie's grasp. He wedged his own grip around the zombie's thumb as the rest of the undead bottom-feeders tugged at his clothes, pulling him down farther.

Zack felt the burn in his lungs, running out of air. He pulled back the zombie's thumb as hard as he could and heard an underwater pop that released Olivia from her zombie anchor. Olivia kicked wildly and shot upward above his head. Zack planted the sole of his shoe on the face of the undead underwater beast tugging at his pant leg and propelled himself upward as well.

A second later, Zack exploded to the surface, gasping for air.

"That was a pretty close one," Olivia said, treading water next to Zack. "You all right?"

"Yeah, I'm okay," Zack said, knocking some excess water out of his ear.

"Okay, guys," Rice called from the pool deck. "Free swim's over!" He pointed skyward to the top of the Double Helix. Up above, Uncle Conrad was already spiraling down the enormous mega-slide.

Zack and Olivia swam frantically for their lives to the side of the pool where Zoe, Madison, Ozzie, and Rice cheered them on and then helped to lift them out of the water onto the cement deck.

SPLASH!

Uncle Conrad torpedoed into the pool and floundered for a moment before doggy-paddling slowly toward the edge of the zombified landing pool.

"Ha!" Rice scoffed. "Look at him. He can hardly swim!"

"Rice!" Madison shouted. "We gotta get out of here!"

CHAPTER 16

The main plaza of the theme park looked like the eye of a zombie hurricane. All around, the zombie hordes were marching like drones back toward the epicenter of Fun World.

"Over here!" Olivia pointed to the hotel facade shaped like a gumball machine rising out of downtown Fun World. "If we can make it up there, we can hitch a ride on the monorail!"

At the other end of the thoroughfare, Cousin Ben was now scooting around in one of the Fun World golf carts, herding the zombie hordes toward the kids.

The kids beelined for the entrance of Hotel Bunco

and raced through the silver doors. Inside the zombified lobby, they rushed past the front desk and veered left until they came to a bank of elevators.

As they waited for an elevator to arrive, a pack of elderly zombies stormed around the corner, shuffling toward them along the black-and-white-checkered linoleum.

"Too-day," Zoe said, tapping her foot impatiently while she watched the elevator numbers above the door light up.

"It's here!" Madison squealed when the elevator dinged. Zoe stepped in front of the elevator next to her as the doors slid open.

"*Blargh!*" A dense cluster of undead elevator riders charged out at them.

"Ahhhhh!" the girls screamed and turned to run away.

"Come on," Zack cried over the wailing zombie moans. "We have to take the stairs!"

Racing through the door to the darkened stairwell, Zack looked back and caught a glimpse of super zombie

Cousin Ben and his legion following hot on their trail.

The door closed securely behind Zack, but he couldn't see a thing in the pitch-dark stairwell. The lights had blacked out and the smell of rotting zombie flesh saturated the heavy air.

"Hurry up, guys." Ozzie's voice echoed off the walls. "We got zombies coming."

Cloaked in darkness, Zack followed the sound of Ozzie's voice, walking blindly up the steps. "We need to get to the seventh floor for monorail access," Olivia said.

"I can't see where I'm going," Madison complained.

"EEEK!" Zack heard Olivia squeal, followed by two loud smacks and a booming *thwack*.

"What just happened?" Zack asked.

"I think Ozzie just took

down a zombie on pure ninja sense alone," said Rice with awe in his voice.

"Yeah," Ozzie said. "That and it also helps to have night-vision goggles handy."

"Well played, Oz," said Zack.

"Okay, buddy," Ozzie said to Zack. "You're going to need to duck right now."

"Huh?"

"Duck!" Ozzie shouted.

Zack crouched down fast and heard Ozzie blast the zombie behind him in the stomach with his Slugger. *THUMP-THUMP-THUMP*. The zombie stairwell dweller went tumbling down the steps. With the zombie

out of the way, Zack shot up the stairs but slipped on a trail of slime coating one of the steps. About to flail backward, he felt Ozzie's hand grab him by the wrist and drag him after the others on their way to the seventh floor.

"Nice save," Zack said, putting his arm on Ozzie's shoulder. "Thanks."

"It was nothing," Ozzie's voice said out of the darkness.

A flight above, Zoe hustled up the darkened steps. "Go, go, go!" she yelled to Rice.

"Stop pushing me!" Rice yelled back.

"Stop yelling!" Madison and Olivia both shouted.

"Through that door!" Ozzie yelled.

"What door?"

"This one." The door flung open, casting a bright triangle of moonlight into the stairwell, shining from a hallway window. A herd of shadowy zombies rounded down from the staircase above them. Zack and the gang followed the light onto the seventh floor and shut the door behind them. Ozzie took off his night-vision goggles and slipped them back in his pack.

In front, Zack ran through the halls, dodging through a gauntlet of hotel zombie freaks rampaging in and out of the demolished hotel rooms. He made a left underneath a sign overhead directing them to the waiting deck for the Fun World monorail. A digital board dripping in slime told him the next train would be coming in three minutes, but they had only about thirty seconds before the hotel zombies would converge on them in the close quarters of the corridor.

With Madison, Zoe, Rice, Olivia, Twinkles, and Ozzie right behind him, Zack sprinted past the monorail platform and through the melee to the stairwell on the other side of the floor.

They tried to go down, but the zombies were already coming up, so they quickly turned the other way. Climbing the last flight of stairs, they burst through the access door into a short hallway with two elevators and a single locked door marked with a P on the wall above the lock.

Behind them, the elevator doors dinged shut and the elevator cars descended to the lower floors.

"The super zombies must be calling the elevators back down!" Madison shouted.

"We're trapped!" Zoe yelled. Madison banged on the double doors of the penthouse, screaming for someone to let them in.

Suddenly, the door to the stairwell flung open and a stray, mammoth zombie man plowed right into Ozzie. It was shirtless and blubbery, sweaty and savagely snarling with slime-caked fur all over its bare, flabby torso.

"Oomph," Ozzie huffed, and put his hand up to shield himself from the undead monster's chomping maw, but the zombie shifted his head to the left and bit down hard on Ozzie's fingers with a crunch.

"Yow!" Ozzie howled an awful, pain-stricken yowl and struck down the ghoul with a swift leg kick to its stomach. "It got me! The sonofagun got me!" He waved his arm around, showing off his bloody finger.

Ozzie groaned, clutching his zombie-bitten pinky, and collapsed on the ground as the zombie virus moved quickly through his bloodstream.

"Let's try to get him inside there!" yelled Madison,

and she and Olivia moved to drag him toward another penthouse door at the end of the hall.

Zack pulled hard on the door, but it too was locked tight.

Ozzie lay on the floor, slipping in and out of consciousness.

"Ozzie!" Rice shouted as he held him by the collar with two hands. "You have to tell us how to pick this lock."

"That's all right, Santa," he said woozily. "All Ozzie wants for Christmas is a new set of nunchucks."

"Nunchaku," Zoe corrected.

"Have some compassion, Zoe," Rice said. "He's zombifying!"

At the end of the hall, the elevators reopened and a flock of sweaty, undead goons stumbled out. The other elevator car dinged, too, and another pack of zombies stormed into the hallway.

"Get out of the way, Zack." Olivia pushed him aside, plucking an ATM card out of her wallet and a bobby pin out of her hair. "I've only done this

once before so no promises, but here goes. . . ." She slid the plastic card in the crack of the door by the lock and jiggled the bobby pin inside the lock itself.

Behind them, the mass of misshapen corpses limped lamely up the hallway.

"*Al-most* got it," Olivia said, jiggling the pin in the lock.

The gangly procession of undead maniacs howled bloody murder, their lips stained rum-red with blood. Zack ran up to the first wave of zombies staggering off the elevators and wielded his bat, conking out two undead noggins with a single mighty swing.

"There!" Olivia shouted, and the door to the hotel suite flew open at the last second.

Zack backed away from the oncoming herd of zombies while Zoe and Madison dragged Ozzie into the plush foyer of the penthouse suite and laid him out on the living room floor. Then Zack, Rice, and Olivia all piled in next and pushed the doors shut on the converging swarm in the hall.

"Quick!" Zack shouted. "We have to barricade the door!"

Zack, Zoe, Madison, and Olivia began to pull over as many sofas and chairs as they could find and push them up against all the doors to make solid barriers. Rice went over to check on Ozzie, whose head was slumped to the side with a little blob of drool dripping from the corner of his mouth.

Behind them, a tall lanky figure hobbled out of the shadows and looked down at the kids.

"Aww, man, I thought they were all out there!" said Olivia, turning around.

Rice gazed up at the man. "That's not a zombie," he said with awe in his voice. He turned to the rest of the gang. "That's a Bunco!"

A loud cough reverberated through the office as the big Bunkowski stepped into view. He was tall, nearly six

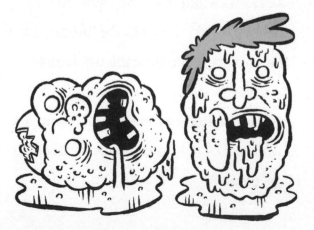

foot six, and had a thinning head of white fluffy hair and a thick white mustache that connected to his white mutton-chop sideburns. Bunco had on leather sandals and khaki shorts with a pink polo shirt. One of his legs was the kind of regular appendage you'd expect from a man his size and breadth, but the other was a mechanical prosthetic that gave him a hitch in his step. His shoulders were narrow and his hips were wide, giving him the appearance of a pear or some kind of Halloween gourd, skinny side up.

"Greetings," he said, standing before them. "My name is RJ Bunkowski, but you can call me Bunco."

"Mr. Bunco." Rice stepped forward, putting his hand out to shake. "It's a real honor to meet you, sir! I'm a big admirer of your life's work."

"The pleasure's all mine, Johnston," Bunco said.

Rice's eyes widened. "He knows my name?"

"Big whoop," said Zoe as she turned to address Bunco. "Have you been up here the whole time?"

"Well, I wasn't going down there. Look what happened." Bunco laughed nervously and pointed at Ozzie sprawled on the floor. "I don't want to become one of those things again."

"You used to be a zombie?"

Bunco nodded yes.

"Join the club," Madison said.

"But you haven't rezombified?"

"What does 'rezombified' mean?"

"That's what's happening," Zack informed him. "Everyone who got unzombified by the original popcorn antidote is rezombifying back to their previous undead state!"

"Wow," said Bunco. "That's heavy, man! All I know is that before the last outbreak, I took a bite of a BurgerDog and woke up with two busted wrists and a leg missing, but that one bite was the single most delightful flavor-tasting experience of my life. I even did a tribute to the popcorn/brain flavoring that saved us all. Would you like to try one? I have a sample in my study."

"Does a zombie eat brains in the woods?" Rice asked as they all followed him into the next room.

The funny-looking fellow walked behind his desk to one of the many glass jars on the shelves lining the walls top to bottom, each one seeming to be filled with a different flavor gumball, and selected one for each of the kids.

Madison and Olivia both squinched up their faces in revulsion. "No thanks."

"I'm good," said Zack.

Rice took one of the gumballs from Bunco's hand and popped it in his mouth. "Mmmmm," he said, chewing the brain-flavored popcorn ball. "You know," he said. "People throw the word 'genius' around a lot these days. But you, sir, are a true visionary. Your own amusement park. Your own bubble gum factory. Your own cruise ship. Your own brand of energy drink—"

"We even have gumballs infused with that, too! Our new Spazola flavors are raspberry-lemon, kiwi-strawberry, and blackberry-cherry. Ooh, and we now have a specialty line of flavors for the practical jokers out there: gumballs that taste like the inside of an old shoe, ones that taste like dirty laundry. . . . Would you care to try one?"

"Uh . . . let me try one of those Spazola-infused ones," said Rice, eyeing the multicolored glass jars. "Blackberry-cherry, please." Bunco handed Rice a gumball and Rice popped it in his mouth. "This is the greatest thing I've ever tasted—"

"Oh, please," Zoe said. "How can you be thinking about gumballs at a time like this?" She smacked Rice in the back of his head, making him choke and swallow the yummy gumball he was chewing.

"Not cool, Zoe," he said. "Do you know how long it takes chewing gum to get out of your system? Like seven years!"

"I've heard you can never get it out," Madison said, stretching a piece of chewed gum out of her mouth until it snapped.

A light bulb flashed in Zack's head. "That's it! We

want to make the antidote permanent, right?" he said. "Well, what if we put the antidote in the gumballs? It'll last at least seven years." He turned to Bunco. "You have a factory around here, right?"

"Yes," said Bunco. "It's less than a mile from here. I'll take you myself. With your antidote and my gumballs, we can unzombify everything for good. All we have to do is add the antidote into the mixer. The rest is automated." Bunco pressed a special button on his desk and turned back to the kids. "I just called the monorail to come pick us up. We can access it through my secret passageway." He pressed another button and the study wall opened, revealing a small corridor. "Man, is anyone else hot in here?"

Bullets of sweat streamed down his brow, and Zack

could see the great bubble gum baron's eyes start to dilate and his skin begin to turn a shade of mucus green.

"Back up, everybody!" Zack yelled. "Bunco's about to bite the big one!"

"Urgh!" Bunco let out a loud groan and grabbed his belly as if he was having an intense and sudden stomach cramp. Then he moaned even louder and collapsed down on his one good knee.

As Bunco writhed on the floor in the throes of his pre-rezombification, Ozzie Briggs awoke from his zombie slumber in the living room and shot off the floor completely zombified.

"*Blargh!*" he roared, coming into Bunco's office. Zack and Rice tackled zombie Ozzie to the ground and quickly gave him a dose of ginkgo. Olivia pulled over a rolling office chair and the boys sat him up as he fell into a ginkgo zombie stupor.

Behind them, the door burst open and the zombies who had been pushing and clawing at the doors barreled through.

Zack rolled Ozzie away from the undead swarm over to the girls now waiting by Bunco's private monorail access. Bunco was rolling around on the floor convulsing in thick puddles of drool. Rice rushed for Bunco, but Zack pulled him back. "Bunco!" Rice cried, trying to shake loose, but it was no use.

"It's too late for him now!" Zack yelled over the shriek and groan of the zombie penthouse trashers. "We gotta get outta here, man!"

They dashed through Bunco's secret passageway leading to the Fun World monorail and caught up with the girls.

"Guys, we need a code for this thing," said Madison, referring to the keypad-activated lock leading to the monorail.

Zack raced back to the study doorway. The stinking mass of decomposing bodies had filled up the suite to maximum capacity. "Bunco!" he shouted to the old gumball guru. "We need the code! What's the code?"

Bunco's rezombifying head turned, gazing at Zack. The life was rushing from his face and his eyes had a far-off look, but there seemed to be a tiny spark left. "Gumballs," Bunco said deliriously, and then passed out.

The zombies funneled through the study doorway, gargling phlegm and flailing their arms, thrashing across the floor.

"What did he say?" asked Zoe.

"All he said was 'gumballs,'" Zack said, bewildered.

"Well, there's only numbers," Zoe said, gesturing toward the keypad.

"Maybe do it like a telephone," Madison said. "48622557."

Zoe punched in the code, and the passageway opened to a platform for the Fun World monorail system.

"OMG," Zoe said to her BFF. "That was, like, so smart of you."

"Thanks. I thought so, too," said Madison as they all boarded the waiting monorail car, dragging zombie Ozzie in his whirly chair behind them.

"Next stop: visitor parking," a digitized voice recording announced over the loudspeaker, and the monorail took off into the warm Florida night.

CHAPTER 17

The Fun World monorail zipped off toward the parking lot, high above the zombie mayhem on the ground below.

Rice was pouting in the backseat. "I can't believe we lost Bunco. I had so many questions I wanted to ask him."

"Look on the bright side," said Zack. "At least he gave us instructions. And we've got Olivia. And Bunco knew who we were."

"Well," said Rice, "he knew who *I* was."

"Whatever," said Zack.

"He's not gone forever," Madison consoled Rice.

"You guys are right," said Rice, perking up a little.

"Cuz we're going to fix the antidote. Then we can unzombify him, and I can ask him anything I want."

The sleek aboveground train glided along the track, buzzing with electromagnetic propulsion. Zack pulled out Ozzie's binoculars and peered at Fun World below them. A gigantic zombie swarm was pouring out of the gates and surging into the parking lot. Super zombies Uncle Conrad, Aunt Ginny, and Cousin Ben were all now driving the go-karts, herding their seemingly endless supply of zombie minions.

"Whoa," Zack said. "They're still following us!"

A minute later, the monorail ride came to a smooth stop, and the kids hurried onto the platform. Zack pushed zombie Ozzie in the whirly chair as fast as he could. *CLACK!* The front wheel of the desk chair hit a bump in the ground and zombie Ozzie went flying onto the platform floor. Rice, Madison, Zoe, and Olivia were already taking an abandoned escalator to the ground, so Zack picked Ozzie up off the ground and tossed him back into his seat. "There you go, buddy!" Zack grunted and then raced them down into the Fun World parking lot.

The super zombies led their gigantic swarm of Fun World zombies through the rows of vehicles, trudging in the humidity, their faces pocked and spackled with necrotic decay.

The kids all ducked down as the go-karts zipped through the rows of parked cars. Once they'd passed, Zack and the gang stood behind Olivia as she scratched her head, looking for her parent's rental Jeep. "I thought they'd parked it right over there, but now I don't see it."

"Dude," Rice cried out to Zack. "Behind you!"

Zack spotted the blur of aggressive zombie movement out of the corner of his eye and spun around.

The undead beast swiped at him with its bony claws,

but Zack ducked and hopped to the side as the zombie bent down sinisterly to thrash him with its disgusting septic fingernails. Zack swung his bat and clubbed the rezombified mutant on the back of the head and the thing dropped to the ground in a motionless heap.

"I see it!" Olivia called out, pointing toward the Jeep.

Zoe took off running, dodging zombies sprawled on car rooftops, and reached the Jeep first.

"Here," Olivia said, catching up and tossing Zoe the keys. Zoe jumped in the driver's seat and Olivia hopped in the passenger's side. Zack, Rice, and Madison loaded Ozzie into the storage compartment of the Jeep and then piled in the back.

Zoe turned the ignition key and the engine hummed to life. She hit the gas and the back wheels spun and kicked up dust behind them as they sped through the zombified parking lot.

"Okay, Zoe," Olivia said, looking at her phone as they drove down the highway. "I think you want to make a left just up ahead."

Zack looked out the back window as they cruised off toward the bubble gum factory. In the distance, the go-kart-driving super zombies herded their undead rebellion after them in a slow but steady pursuit.

CHAPTER 18

Speeding toward the bubble gum factory, Zack slumped back in his seat and watched the palm trees whizz by one by one. The warm breeze cooled the sweat on his face, and it felt good not to worry, if only for a second, about some zombic freak trying to bite him.

"Ugh!" Rice clutched his stomach in the backseat.

Zack looked at his pal, who grimaced back. "You okay, man?" he asked.

"I think I'm okay." Rice belched. "No thanks to Zoe making me swallow that bubble gum. That . . . or the Funyuns. It could have definitely been all the Funyuns."

He groaned. "The bubble gum plus the Funyuns." Rice's stomach grumbled audibly.

A short while later, they pulled off the boulevard and coasted up the driveway to Bunco Inc. Streaks of slime crisscrossed the blacktop and the sidewalk in front of the building. The air was a fetid mix of septic stink and rainbow fruit flavors. Twin smokestacks churned out two clouds of the sweet-smelling exhaust, which wafted through the undead Florida fog like cheap air freshener in a public restroom.

"This is it," Zoe said, slowing the Jeep to a stop. "We're here."

Zack and the gang hopped out and strolled up to the main entrance. Rice rolled zombie Ozzie up the handicap ramp in the chair from Bunco's office. On the sidewalk, two abandoned cars were T-boned in front of the entrance, and two trails of zombie slime were coming from each driver's seat.

As they pushed inside, the facility was silent but for the clanking, ambient sound of industrial machinery reverberating throughout the whole place.

They made their way down the hallway, and just as they turned the corner, two zombified factory workers wearing bright yellow overalls and protective eyewear lunged out from the adjacent corridor.

"Glarph!" The zombies gargled on their half-swallowed tongues. They were both big and oafish, and the collars of their white Bunco Inc. T-shirts were covered in green-black filth.

Zoe leaped in the air and jump-kicked an undead lummox right in the buttocks.

"Hi-ya!" she yelled as she delivered the blow. The zombie's whole hip gave way and he collapsed to the side.

"Ahhhhh!" Olivia shrieked as the second zombie brute grabbed her tightly by the hair. She reached above her head and grabbed the undead hair-puller by the wrist with both hands, then twisted around and pried the factory-worker zombie's fingers off her hair. "Back up!" she yelled at the zombie and then landed two power punches to its midsection. The beast wheezed out a batch of hot, stinking breath and crumpled to the ground from the body blow.

Suddenly, zombie Ozzie woke up from his ginkgo nap and lurched out of his rolling chair, going straight for Rice.

"Rargh!" Ozzie clenched his two zombified hands around Rice's throat, nearly strangling him.

"Dude," Rice squawked, "I'm sorry I lost your nunchaku."

"Nunchargha!" Ozzie bellowed, about to chomp right into Rice's skull.

"No!" Zack cried as his zombie buddy went in for the bite. Zack whacked Ozzie in the side of the head with the baseball bat just hard enough, and zombie Ozzie dropped to the cold, hard floor with a clunk.

"Sorry, Oz," said Zack, backing away from his unconscious zombie friend.

"Don't worry about him," said Rice. "He'll be fine; he's a zombie."

At the other end of the hallway, a pack of factory-worker zombies turned the corner and came waddling toward the kids.

"Come on, dorkbrains," said Zoe. "We gotta find out where to make the gumballs!"

They plopped zombie Ozzie's conked-out body back in the whirly chair and sprinted down a connecting hallway that had a sign that read: GUMBALL PRODUCTION ⇨. In the middle of the hall, Zack leaned on the door marked RESTRICTED ACCESS ONLY, opening it slightly. A stream of slime slithered down the door, and a surge of round, white eyeballs with squiggly red veins and blue-black pupils rolled out at his feet.

"Yuck!" Madison squealed. "Eyeballs!"

"They're not eyeballs," said Rice, picking one up. "They're gumballs!"

As the mass of candy eyeballs spread out around them, two zombie swarms appeared, one at each end of the hallway.

"Ew, Twinkles," said Madison as her pup picked up an eyeball gumball in his mouth. "Drop it!" But Twinkles wouldn't listen and started to chew the gumball. Madison raced over to him and bent down, but Twinkles backed up with a little growl. Madison grabbed him and stuck her fingers in his mouth, pulling out the chewable eyeball. "OMG," she said, holding the slimy orb in between her fingers. "It's a real one!" She squealed and threw the actual eyeball down the hallway. "Bad Twinkles!"

Zack leaned his shoulder against the door again, but he could push it open only a few more inches. He squinted one eye and peeked inside the production facility. The machines were going full throttle, churning out the eyeball gumballs, which had accumulated about three feet high off the ground.

"Well," said Rice, peeking over Zack's shoulder, "at least we know the equipment's working. . . ."

"Quick," Zack said. "Help me shovel some of these things out." He bent down and stuck his arm into the room, scooping out the gumball overflow from the production floor.

The girls kicked heaps of the eyeball gumballs down each end of the corridor.

As the gumballs rolled down the hall and hit the zombies' feet, the front lines of undead factory workers started to slip and topple on their dislocated knees and ankles.

"Okay, Come on!" Zack shouted.

The five of them shimmied inside the production facility, dragging zombie Ozzie behind them.

Once inside, Zack could see what was going on.

Though all the bubble gum factory employees had rezombified, the factory had been automatically churning out eyeball gumballs for the past forty-eight hours. In front of him, Rice, Zoe, Madison, and Olivia waded through the waist-high pile of gumballs like they were in a Chuck E. Cheese ball pit.

Giant stainless steel tanks towered above the eyeball-covered ground, and silver chutes slanted at all angles out of the heavy-duty bubble gum mixers. The metallic machinery glimmered in the moonlight that shone through twin-arched windows looking out over the Florida coast.

"Okay, guys," Zack said, kicking a few hundred more gumballs out into the hallway so he could close the door. "We need to zombie-proof ourselves in here until we can mass-produce the antidote."

"But first we need to shut down production on eyeball gumballs and get some of these brain-flavored gumballs cooking," Rice said.

"Hey, look over here," Madison said, getting everyone's attention. "There's some kind of control room over there."

"Cool," said Zack. "What are we waiting for?"

They all treaded through the gumball ball pit and gathered inside the control room. It reminded Zack of the BurgerDog factory at the end of the first outbreak. Like the zombie nightmare was almost over.

"Step one." Rice hit the reset button on the control panel and the gumball production line slowed to a stop. "Step two," Rice said as he adjusted the settings to produce a batch of popcorn/brain-flavored gumballs. "Now all we have to do is add in the antidote when we start the mixer and voilà—"

"Dude, what are you doing?" Zack asked. "How do you know all this?"

"When I wrote my paper on Bunco, Mrs. Gordon only gave me a C plus," Rice said, flicking a couple more switches. "So for extra credit, I wrote her another paper on Bunco's bubble gum–making process. And on that, my friend, I got an A minus."

Rice looked at the computer monitor and checked the preset ingredients then went back out to the factory floor. They followed Rice over to the mixer and watched him add a few dashes of Olivia's antidote serum. "Now we're ready," said Rice as he pulled back the start lever and the gears began to crank once again.

"Nice work, bro," Zack said, high-fiving his boy.

"Just trying to make up for the whole super zombie thing," he said.

Nearby, zombie howls could be heard over the noise of the automatic machinery churning out the batch of antidote gumballs.

They rushed to the high arching windows and peered out onto the factory grounds. A mind-boggling mass of Fun World zombies was converging on the gumball factory.

"There's so many of them," Olivia remarked as they watched more and more Floridian freakazoids join the Fun World crowd from the surrounding area.

"Why are they all coming here?" asked Zoe.

"They're attracted to the smell," said Zack.

MIXER

He was referring to the factory smokestacks emitting the hybrid scent of brains and popcorn into the air outside.

As the doomsday zombie swarm reached Bunco's production facility, they laid siege to the bubble gum factory, crashing through the gates.

"Hurry up, guys. We need to make sure the gumball antidote works!" Rice shouted to Zack as the first of the antidote gumballs was ready. "Test it out on Ozzie."

Zack stuffed one of the gray gumballs into Ozzie's unconscious zombie mouth and watched it slide down his throat in a single involuntary gulp.

In an instant, Ozzie's eyes popped open and he jumped to his feet.

"Back up!" Zack shouted to the rest of them, and they all edged away from the unzombifying martial arts master. "Give him some room."

Ozzie began to spin and cried out one last zombie howl while kicking and jabbing at anything in his general vicinity.

A moment later, Ozzie collapsed in the pit of eyeball

gumballs on the ground, still writhing around wildly like a zombie.

"Uh, Rice," Zack said. "Is that what he's supposed to be doing?"

"Just give it a sec, bro," Rice responded. "I got this one."

Zack turned his attention back to zombie Ozzie and watched him open his eyes. He gazed down at Ozzie's face, checking to see if he was all right.

"Yo." Ozzie yawned loudly, shaking off his undead grogginess. "What's up?"

They all cheered and lifted their unzombified buddy off the ground. But there was no time to celebrate. The zombies were here.

CHAPTER

WHAM! BOOM! Furious blow after furious blow from the Floridian zombies shook the fire escape door on the factory floor. The door flung open and Olivia's super zombie brother burst inside. Cousin Ben scampered nimbly down the wrought iron ladder and hopped onto the eyeball-gumball-covered production floor with a grunt.

Then the main door leading to the factory thumped and pounded with the force of a thousand undead fists. *POW!* The hallway door blasted open and super zombie Aunt Ginny plowed inside, too.

BANG! CRACK!

One of the twin arched windows shattered and a shower of glass shards crashed to the floor. Zack swiveled his head to the noise as super zombie Uncle Conrad appeared in the window frame. At the base of the window, Zack could see a roiling mass of zombified arms, legs, and heads writhing beneath the super zombie's feet. Outside the factory, the Fun World zombies had been piled on top of one another until they'd formed a humongous staircase of the rotting undead. Standing atop his massive heap of rezombified minions, Uncle Conrad glared down into the gumball factory.

Uncle Conrad stepped off his undead escalator and jumped down onto the catwalk below the window, then bounded into the pit of gumballs to join his wife and son.

"They look pretty hungry," Rice said.

Zack carried over a bucket of the antidote gumballs while Rice produced two Fun World slingshots from his backpack. "Brain-flavored, antidote-infused gumballs with a slight popcorn glaze."

Madison and Twinkles stood guard in front of Olivia

while Ozzie and Zoe each clutched an antidote gumball in one hand and moved forward to try to get within range of the super zombies.

Zack and Rice started firing off rounds of the antidote gumballs with their Fun World slingshots, just missing the super zombies' mouths and smacking them in their heads.

Aunt Ginny power walked through the floor of eyeball gumballs, gurgling black bile in the back of her throat with her mouth wide open.

The brain-flavored popcorn antidote gumballs whizzed by her head as Zack and Rice fired away until one of the gumballs made a direct hit and nailed the little ding-dong thing at the back of the super zombie's throat.

"Yes!" Rice pumped his fist. "One to nothing!"

"No way," Zack protested. "I totally shot that gumball!"

"In your dreams," said Rice. "One zip."

"Glugh-glugh-glargh!" Super zombie Aunt Ginny whirled around, squawking and choking before falling face-first into the pit of eyeball gumballs.

Zack and Rice lowered their slingshots and prepared to reload.

"Take a break, fellas," Ozzie said. "I think this sucker's going to need to get force-fed."

Ozzie approached super zombie Uncle Conrad, and the two of them squared off like boxers at the starting bell. Uncle Conrad's clammy, white, pupil-less eyeballs bulged out of his sunken yellow cheeks.

Ozzie made the first move and bum-rushed Uncle Conrad, trying to slam the gumball into the super zombie's mouth. The ghoul gagged and spat it out, then slammed Ozzie to the ground and roared, fangs of spittle hanging from his toothy maw.

Zack pulled back the slingshot and lined it up to Olivia's pop's wide-open gullet. He plucked his fingers like an archer launching an arrow from his bow and let the gumball fly. The brain-flavored antidote gumball sailed through the air and right into the zombie's mouth.

"All tied up," Zack said to Rice, who then gave him a respectful fist bump.

Uncle Conrad glugged down the gumball antidote with a confused look on his super zombie face. Ozzie hopped up off the ground and clocked the super ghoul in the noggin. Uncle Conrad crumpled in the waist-high pit of eyeball gumballs.

Over the cranking of the factory's machinery they could still hear the never-ending zombie onslaught coursing through the hallways of the factory like an infection through the bloodstream.

"You guys, we got Aunt Ginny and Uncle Conrad," Zack said. "Where's Ben?"

"Blargh!"

Olivia's super zombie brother rose out of the gumball pit directly behind Zack.

Zack spun a hundred and eighty degrees and faced off one-on-one with Cousin Ben. "Easy, tiger."

Olivia's super zombie brother chuckled to himself with animal glee and faked a lunge at his prey. Zack flinched and stumbled backward as the maniacal super-freak cackled once again and then pounced in a flash.

Zack dropped his shoulder at the oncoming hellion, bracing for the hit. Cousin Ben raised his pale white forearms popping with purple veins high in the air and wrapped Zack up in a super zombie bear hug. They both went toppling sidelong into the waist-level gumball quicksand.

Zack squiggled free from the super zombie's tight arm-flexing grip around his waist and kicked back behind himself like a perturbed donkey. He kicked a second time, and the sole of his sneaker made a direct hit on super zombie Ben's undead forehead, imprinting a waffle-iron pattern into his pale, wrinkly flesh. Zack scrabbled to his feet as Olivia's super zombie brother grumbled and slunk into the pool of eyeball gumballs.

They all breathed a sigh of relief until Aunt Ginny suddenly rose back up and started groaning and lurching like a zombie, even though she had swallowed the antidote.

"Mom?" Olivia asked.

Then Uncle Conrad, who had just swallowed the antidote, rose up again, too. "Dad?" Olivia turned to her super zombie father.

Conrad breathed heavily, his eyes seething with furious delirium. He opened his gangrenous mouth and let forth a cantankerous roar.

"What the heck?" Rice said, his eyes wide with fear.

"The antidote isn't working on them," Zack said.

"What do you mean the antidote isn't working?" Zoe quickly scrambled up from the eyeball-gumball-covered floor. "It worked on Ozzie, so it should be working on these guys."

"Okay, so maybe it only works on regular zombies?" Madison guessed.

Immune to the effects of the antidote, Aunt Ginny and Uncle Conrad marched through the gumball pit toward Ozzie, who stood in his kung fu stance between them and his friends.

"I'll handle the super zombies," said Ozzie. "You guys start using the antidote on the regular zombies. Let's try to save some lives, people."

As Olivia's undead parents approached, Ozzie dove down and disappeared beneath the sea of gumballs. Before the super zombies could make sense of it, Ozzie emerged behind them then grabbed both of their heads at the same time and clunked them together as hard as he could. Uncle Conrad and Aunt Ginny slumped into the gumball heap and sank below the surface once again.

"You guys," said Zoe, pointing toward the factory door where a densely packed herd of zombies were pouring in. "We've got bigger problems than a couple of super zombies not un-super-zombifying."

CHAPTER

The Fun World zombies from the hallway stormed in through the door to the production floor, slowly but surely wading through the swamplike volume of eyeball gumballs.

As Ozzie rejoined the gang, Zack and Rice scooped up a few buckets full of antidote gumballs and lugged them to within range of the zombie swarm. The others quickly formed an assembly line starting at the tank of antidote gumballs and started passing industrial-sized buckets full of gumballs back and forth to the boys.

The undead beasts gazed at Zack and the gang with looks of pure insatiable gluttony on their revolting faces.

As the zombies lumbered toward the kids, they stuck their decaying arms into the pit, plucking up as many of the eyeball gumballs off the floor as they could and cramming them into their mouths.

"Nom nom nom."

The air around the zombies' heads was now visibly blurry with fumes of shimmering hot stench emanating from the zombie open-mouthed chewing.

Yet before the undead swarm could reach Zack and Rice, and their buckets of antidote gumballs, the zombies began to drop one after the other, collapsing face-first into the pit of candy eyeballs.

"What's going on?" Olivia cried. "They haven't eaten the antidote yet!"

A few moments later, the zombies began to rise again, stretching their arms widely as if they were waking up grumpily from naps and making sounds like they were sucking their own brains through their nostrils and down the backs of their throats. The zombie closest to Zack and Rice had a mean underbite about its muzzle and it glanced around at the kids with a strange glimmer in its eye.

"Oh, man," Zack said. "That's not normal."

"Is that what I think it is?" Madison asked.

"That depends," said Zoc. "Do you think it's a super zombie?"

"Uh-huh." She nodded.

"But how is that possible?" Olivia asked.

"You guys," said Rice, picking up one of the eyeball gumballs from the floor and biting into it. "Bad news. These things aren't just eyeball gumballs. . . . These are the ones infused with Spazola Energy Cola." The words fell off Rice's tongue like gumballs out of a candy machine.

Zack gasped, realizing what his friend meant. He looked around at the accumulated spillage of eyeball gumballs they'd been standing in the entire time and that the zombies, including the one now staring them down, had been munching on.

"Spazballs" was all Zack could say.

"We've got to get out of here," Ozzie said, interrupting their trains of thought. "There's more of those super zombie things waking up!"

"What about my parents?" Olivia asked.

"We'll get you some new parents!" Zoe shrieked, moving away from the super-zombifying horde.

"We can't help them when they're trying to get us," Zack said. "The only way to help them is to leave them behind until we can figure out the new super antidote."

Zoe, Madison, Ozzie, and Rice shouted for Zack and Olivia as the new batch of super zombies waddled and lurched across the production floor's pit of eyeball gumballs. Then they grabbed as many of the popcorn/ brain-flavored antidote gumballs as they could carry and retreated toward the back fire escape.

With Twinkles tucked in Madison's arm, they scaled the fire escape ladder to the platform above.

As they reached the top, Zack saw that the emergency-exit door was torn off its hinges and a dense pack of undead brain-gobblers was shuffling and lurching toward them along the catwalk.

"There's nowhere to go!" Zack shouted.

"Yes there is!" Ozzie said, pointing at the gargantuan staircase of undead freaks still climbing over one another beneath the high arching window of the factory. "That's how Uncle Conrad came in!"

Olivia, Madison, and Zoe peered through the busted window at the gigantic flight of zombies leading from the sill to ground level. "Yeah," the three of them all agreed. "That's like the worst idea of all time!"

"It's better than getting devoured by those dudes!" Rice shouted, pointing toward the thick horde of zombie cretins still lumbering behind them on the narrow catwalk.

Zack stood on the ledge of the broken window and took a deep breath. Below him, a squirming staircase of undead bodies contorted and churned. "Here goes nothing!" he said, and sprinted down the heap of zombies first.

Zack jumped from zombie noggin to zombie noggin, careful to avoid the bright yellow bile dribbling from their slack-jawed mouths. Each ghoul was coated in zombie grime, and Zack had to catch his balance as he wobbled on one zombie's double chin and then bounded off down the writhing mountain of ghouls.

Halfway to the ground, his foot slipped into one of the open-mouthed zombie faces, and before he could take it out, the undead brute chomped down on a whole piece of his sneaker, just missing his toes.

"Aww, man!" Zack yelled, pulling his foot loose. "Watch out for that dude!" he yelled back to his friends behind him.

Zack's pant cuffs were now sopping wet with zombie slime, and he was doing his best to navigate his way, but as he neared the ground, a hand shot out from the heap and caught his ankle. Zack toppled forward and face-planted into the base of the zombie steps, his head dunking straight into a puddle of zombie slime that had accumulated on the ground.

"Yuck!" Zack pried his leg free and then jumped to his feet. He wiped his face clean on his grimy T-shirt and turned around to see how the rest of his friends were doing.

Up above, on the back wall of the factory, a large banner read: COMING SOON! SPAZOLA ENERGY GUMBALLS! On each side of the banner was a graphic of two spazzed-out eyeballs.

Would've been helpful five minutes ago, Zack thought, watching his friends work their way down the humongous hill of contorted flesh-eaters.

Ozzie hopped nimbly from zombie head to zombie head while Rice half slid, half crab-walked down the slippery slope. The girls emitted a constant series of high-pitched squeals as they tumbled and rolled down the zombie incline. Twinkles disappeared midjourney, sliding into a slimy crevasse in the steep zombie slope, but as the rest of them reached the ground, the little pup trotted out covered in sludge. He shook himself clean, sending slime everywhere.

"Okay, now I'm like totally disgusted!" Madison shook the zombie slime off her hands and wiped it on Zoe's shirt.

"Yo, dude," said Zoe. "Don't wipe that zombie slime on me." Zoe then lunged and wiped her slimy hands off in Madison's hair. "No backs!"

"OMG," Madison said. "You so didn't just do that!"

"Ladies!" Zack shouted, gesturing to the roving packs of rezombified flesh-eaters stumbling all across

the Florida landscape. "Can we please go now?"

"Fine," said Madison. "I call truce."

"Normally I don't like truces," said Zoe. "But in this case, I'll make an exception." Madison then pulled out a handful of zombie sludge from her back and smeared it all in her BFF's face. Madison laughed hysterically and took off running for the Jeep.

"Hey, guys," Rice said, looking at his smartphone once they were all in the car. "Bunco has that cruise ship not that far away."

"Rice, this is no time to start planning a vacation," Madison said.

"Yeah," Olivia said. "You super zombified my parents and half of Fun World and now you want to go on a cruise?"

"I have a plan," Rice said. "In order to figure out the super zombie antidote, we have to go to the source. We have to find a live jellyfish specimen so we can do some more tests and figure out how to unzombify these super zombies once and for all."

"A cruise ship might be just what we need," Ozzie said. "There's lots more of those super zombie freaks now, so it's probably a good idea to get off the mainland until we can figure things out."

Zack liked the sound of that. It was time for a break. The zombies weren't going anywhere. That much was certain.

"To the SS *Fun World*." Rice pointed down the road leading toward the Atlantic Ocean.

The moonlight glimmered over Orlando as the Jeep cruised away from the super zombie horror they had created and toward the Florida coast.

Zack slunk down in the backseat and sighed heavily.

The super zombie war had only just begun.

What half-dead decaying super-ghouls will
the Zombie Chasers take on next?
Find out in:

BUT FIRST, TAKE A SNEAK PEEK AT
BOOK 1 OF JOHN KLOEPFER'S
OUT-OF-THIS-WORLDNEW SERIES,

MEET THE CHARACTERS IN

GALAXY'S MOST WANTED

KEVIN BREWER. Science genius. Physics, biology, chemistry—you name it, Kevin can do it. He's the brains of the operation, leader of the crew. And he's not about to let Alexander Russ win this year's Invention Convention.

WARNER REED. Kevin's best friend and resident cool dude. He's the guy to see if you've got a 2 a.m. junk-food craving— but you'll pay top dollar for his top secret stash. Despite his low-key attitude, Warner will go toe-to-toe with the baddest science nerd around any day of the week . . . and totally dominate.

TARA SWIFT. Not only is Tara supersmart and great at building things out of next to nothing, she's also in an all-girl punk band and the best drummer in the universe. (It's true, just ask her.) But seriously, she's probably Kevin's best friend at camp—aside from his BFF Warner, that is.

TJ BOYD. Computer problems? He's your man. TJ's a regular computer-programming prodigy. He's not much of a talker, though. Word around the campfire is that he damaged his voice box in a botched robotics experiment (but Kevin knows that's only gossip).

MIM. This is his first time on earth, and he's discovering so many exciting things: candy bars, spiders (which are pretty tasty), and some great human pals! But an extraterrestrial army is out to kidnap him for his thick, purple fur. Can the kids save their new furry friend before he finds himself on the wrong end of an alien poacher's de-atomizer?